He'd kissed her like he meant it.

Jenna felt like a mask had been pulled off. That he could see straight into the depths of her most private self.

And Drew helped her into the car and gave her a reassuring smile and a friendly wave as the car pulled away, like it was no big deal. As if he hadn't just tongue-kissed her passionately in front of a crowd of photographers and caused an inner earthquake.

She couldn't let her mind stray down this path. She was a means to an end.

It was Drew Maddox's nature to be seductive. He was probably that way with every woman he talked to. He probably couldn't help himself. Not even if he tried.

She had to keep that fact firmly in mind.

All. The. Time.

* * *

His Perfect Fake Engagement by
Shannon McKenna is part of the
Men of Maddox Hill series.

Dear Reader,

Years ago, I was working an absurd variety of administrative jobs in New York City to pay the bills while trying to be a writer and a singer. One of those jobs happened to be for a big architecture firm in midtown Manhattan. As I typed, filed and hauled coffee, one of the architects came to my notice. I'll call him Javier, to protect the innocent. Tall and dark, with shoulder-length luscious black locks and deep, mysterious eyes, a velvet voice, and truckloads of talent. I was too shy to actually speak to the guy, other than to pass on phone messages, but boy, did he make an impression. So it's no wonder that my current hero is the CEO of a big arcitecture firm. It's an homage to sexy architects, wherever they may be.

In *His Perfect Fake Engagement*, my architect CEO hero, Drew Maddox, finds himself mired in a scandal that's risking his career, until his quick-witted sister, Ava, comes up with the perfect scheme...a fake engagement to her friend Jenna Somers.

I hope you like the first installment of Men of Maddox Hill. There's more to come, so be sure to follow me to stay up-to-date on future books in the series! Look for contact links to my socials and my newsletter on my website, shannonmckenna.com.

Happy reading! Let me know what you think!

Warmest wishes,

Shannon McKenna

SHANNON MCKENNA

HIS PERFECT FAKE ENGAGEMENT

HARLEQUIN

DESIRE

DESIRE™

ISBN-13: 978-1-335-23281-6

His Perfect Fake Engagement

Copyright © 2021 by Shannon McKenna

Recycling programs for this product may not exist in your area.

This edition published by arrangement with Harlequin Books S.A.

For questions and comments about the quality of this book, please contact us at CustomerService@Harlequin.com.

Harlequin Enterprises ULC
22 Adelaide St. West, 40th Floor
Toronto, Ontario M5H 4E3, Canada
www.Harlequin.com

Printed in U.S.A.

One

"I was set up."

Experience had taught Drew Maddox to keep his voice even and calm when dealing with his volatile uncle, but nothing was going to help his cause today.

"The damage is the same!" Malcolm Maddox flung the crumpled handful of cheap tabloid magazines he'd been clutching in his fist onto the conference room table. "For anyone who looks at this, you're just a coke-sniffing scoundrel with a taste for eighteen-year-olds! Why in God's name were you at a party at that lowlife degenerate's house in the first place? What in holy hell were you thinking?"

Drew let out a breath, counting down slowly. The photos in the tabloids were of him, sprawled on a couch, shirt ripped open, looking clouded and disoriented, while a young woman in a leather miniskirt, large breasts popping out of her skin-tight silver top, sat astride him.

"I was trying to help a friend," Drew repeated. "She found out that her younger sister was at that party. She couldn't get in herself, but she knew that I used to run with that guy years ago, so she asked me to check up on her sister."

"We were supposed have dinner with Hendrick and Bev tonight," Uncle Malcolm said furiously. "Did that even cross your mind before you got into this mess?"

"I do remember the dinner, yes," Drew said. Hendrick Hill was Malcolm's longtime partner and co-founder of their architecture firm, Maddox Hill. Drew had always liked the guy, uptight and humorless though he usually was.

"Then Bev reads about your drunken orgy at Arnold Sobel's house at her hairdresser's!" Malcolm stabbed the tabloids with his finger. "She sees the CEO of her husband's company in these pornographic pictures. She was horrified, Drew."

"It wasn't a drunken orgy, Uncle, and I never—"

"Sanctimonious bastard," Malcolm growled. "He had nerve, sputtering at me about morals and appearances. As far as Hendrick is concerned, it doesn't matter how many architectural prizes and honors you've won if you can't keep your pants zipped. He thinks you're a liability now, and if he persuades the rest of the board, he has the votes to oust you, no matter what I say."

"I know," Drew said. "But I was set up at that party. Someone played their cards carefully."

Malcolm let out a savage grunt. "You're the one who's playing, from what I can see. And if the board fires you, all of our clients will smell blood in the water. It's humiliating!"

I was set up. He had to stop repeating it. Uncle Malcolm didn't want to hear it, so at this point he'd be better off just keeping his mouth shut.

PR disaster or not, he couldn't have done anything differently. When his friend Raisa found out someone brought her sister Leticia to one of Arnold Sobel's famously depraved parties, she'd been terrified that the younger woman would fall prey to a house full of drunken, drugged-up playboys.

Then Leticia had stopped answering her phone, and Raisa had completely freaked out. If Drew hadn't intervened, she would have forced her way through Arnold's security and into Sobel's party by herself—with a gun.

It would have ended badly. Certainly for Raisa. Maybe for everyone.

Drew couldn't let that happen.

Of course, as he discovered afterward, Leticia had never been at the party at all. He and Raisa had been played. The target had been Drew all along.

But Uncle Malcolm didn't want to hear it.

"I was set up." He knew the words wouldn't help, but he couldn't stop repeating them. "They staged those pictures. The photographer was lying in wait."

"If there's one thing I hate more than a spoiled ass who thinks the world only exists for his pleasure, it's a whiner," his uncle snarled. "Set up, my ass. You're a Marine, for God's sake! Taken down by a pack of half-dressed showgirls?"

Ava, his younger sister, jumped in. "Uncle Malcolm, think about it," she coaxed. "Drew's not a whiner. A rebel and a screwup, maybe, but he always owned it.

And this is so deliberate. The way those girls ambushed him—"

"Doesn't look like an ambush to me. It looks like a damn orgy!"

"Someone's telling you a story, Uncle," Ava insisted. "Don't be a sucker."

"Ha. All I see is that your brother couldn't care less about the reputation and the future of the company I spent my life building! If Hendrick uses his muscle to get the board to remove you as CEO, I can't stop him. So start brushing up your resumé. As of today, you're job hunting. Face Hendrick tonight like a man. He can tell you his decision then. But as for myself, I'm done, boy. Done with your crap."

Uncle Malcolm stomped out of the room, cane thudding. He tried to slam the door for effect, but the expensive hydraulic hinge made it sigh gently closed after him with a delicate click.

Drew leaned forward, rubbing his aching temples. "I'll skip the dinner with Hendrick," he said wearily. "No one needs me there to make that announcement. I've reached my humiliation quota for the day."

"No, don't. That looks like an admission of guilt," Ava said thoughtfully. "You need to come to dinner, Drew. I have an idea."

Drew gave his sister a wary look. "If anything could make me feel worse right now, it's those four words coming out of your mouth."

"Don't be a wuss," Ava scolded. "This place needs you here as CEO. You're the new face of Maddox Hill. Hell, you're the new face of architecture. Nobody else has what it takes to head up all those big carbon sink building projects you got going. You're the one who won the Global Award for Sustainable Architecture, and the AIA COTE Award—"

"You don't need to flog my résumé to me, Av. I know what's on it."

"And the Green Academy competition, and that's just the eco stuff," Ava persisted. "You're, like, Mr. Cross-Laminated-Sustainable-Timber-Is-Our-Future. Maddox Hill can't stay relevant without you. Everyone will line up to thank me eventually. You'll see."

It didn't surprise him that she would think so. His sister had curly blond hair, huge cobalt blue eyes, a drop-dead figure, charisma to burn and a very, very high opinion of herself. She could bend people effortlessly to her will, especially men. He was the only one who could resist her. She was his little sister, after all.

The whole thing was still sinking in. How much he stood to lose today, in one fell swoop. Control of all his design projects, many of which had been years in the making. Most of all, he hated the thought of losing the Beyond Earth Project. He'd put that together with the collaboration of the robotics research arm of the Maddox Hill Foundation, opening up the field to young architects and engineers to problem-solve the obstacles to human habitation on the moon and Mars.

That project would have just rung all of their late father's bells. Dad had been a dreamer.

"I'm not proposing that you charm Hendrick, or even Uncle Malcolm," Ava said. "That's a woman's job. Your fiancée will do the heavy lifting. You just smile and nod."

"What fiancée?" Drew asked, baffled. "I have to find a fiancée before dinner tonight? That's setting the bar high, Av, even for a wild, carousing playboy like me."

"No, big brother, the finding's done for you already. It came to me like a beautiful brain-flash while Uncle Malcolm was ranting. We need to fight this false story, and I have the perfect counter-story. And she happens to be right nearby today, coincidentally!"

"What the hell are you talking about? Who's here?"

"Your future bride," Ava announced.

Drew was struck silent, appalled. "Av, you're joking, right?"

"Nope! A temporary engagement, of course. Just a few months, to get you over the hump. You met her once, when you were on leave from Iraq, remember? You stopped to visit me at my dorm in Seattle. Remember Jenna, my roommate?"

"The little red-blonde with the glasses? The one who dumped a pitcher of sangria all over me?"

"That's the girl. I was supposed to meet up with her for coffee before her Wexler presentation over at the Curtis Pavilion this afternoon, but Uncle Malcolm was in such a tizzy, I had to reschedule so I could calm him down. Not that it helped much."

"What presentation?"

"Jenna's a biomechanical engineer, and she started her own bionics company a few years ago. She designs prosthetic mechanical limbs. Brain activated, artificial nerves, sensory feedback. Real space-age stuff. I have been doing their PR, and she's up for the Wexler Prize for Excellence in Biomedical Engineering. She gave her introductory presentation to the committee today. Her mission is to make affordable, high-functioning mechanical arms available to everyone who needs one. She's brilliant, she's focused, she cares…in short, she's perfect."

"But why?" He shook his head, baffled. "Why would she do this for me? And why would anyone buy it? And what the hell is the point?"

"They will buy it, and they will love it," Ava said. "Underestimate me at your peril, bro. I am a genius."

"I don't want to tell a pack of lies," Drew said. "It makes me tense."

"You have to fight fire with fire," Ava told him sternly. "You'd rather just give in and torpedo Uncle Malcolm's company rather than try something bold and risky? Someone is pushing a fake story about you. That you're a spoiled, entitled asshat who uses and discards vulnerable young women. Ouch. My story is much better. Handsome bad boy, redeemed by love, his social conscience shocked to life—"

"I have a social conscience already," he growled. "I'm not a complete tool."

"Shh, I'm just brainstorming. The cynical rogue with the secret hunger in his heart who falls for the smart girl in glasses. Humbled by the power of love. Oh, yeah."

"Secret hunger in my heart?" Drew tilted an eyebrow. "Really, Av?"

"Just roll with it, bro. This woman is making artificial arms for people so they can hug their kids again. See where I'm going? Pathos. Warmth. Connection. We all crave it."

"I get it just fine, and you're still nuts," Drew said.

Ava picked her tablet up from the table and tapped the screen a few times, passing it to Drew. "This is Jenna. I had my assistant go over to the Curtis to record her presentation to the Wexler Prize committee, and he already sent me the video. Take a look."

In the video, a young woman was spotlighted on the

circular stage at the Curtis Pavilion, one of the newest high-profile Seattle skyscrapers that Drew had designed. She wore a microphone headset. A sleek fitted short gray dress. She had nice legs. Her strawberry blond ringlets were twisted up into an explosive messy bun, ringlets sproinging out in every direction. She still wore glasses, but now they were cat-eye style, the frames a bright neon green.

Drew held up the tablet. The camera zoomed in on her face. The pointed chin, the tilted hazel eyes. A sprinkle of freckles. Her mouth was full, with a sexy dip in the pillowy softness of her lower lip. Painted hot, glossy red. He tapped the tablet for the sound.

"...new nerve connections, opening the doorways to actual sensations," she was saying, in a low, musical voice. "Holding a paintbrush. Braiding a child's hair. Dribbling a basketball. We take these things for granted, and don't see them for the daily miracles that they are. I want these daily miracles in arm's reach for everyone. Thank you."

There was enthusiastic applause. He muted it. Ava took her tablet back.

"Her company is called Arm's Reach," Ava said. "She's won a bunch of awards already. Most recently the AI and Robotics International Award. That one was a million bucks. But she needs more, to develop ways for people to access the specialized nerve surgery that goes with some of her tech." Ava paused. "She's cute, too. Though I'm sure you noticed."

"Av, I'm sure this woman is too busy helping people with real problems to participate in your little theater project to solve mine," Drew said absently, still gazing down at the tablet. "Send me that video."

"Sure thing." A smile curved Ava's mouth as she swiped and tapped the screen. "Done." She picked up the phone on the table. "Mrs. Crane?" she said. "Is Ms. Somers there? Excellent. Yes, bring her in. Thanks so much."

"Jenna Somers is here, now?" Drew was alarmed. "Ava, I never agreed to—"

"Don't be silly. She's here right now, Drew. What's the point of wasting any time? Hers or ours?" A knock sounded on the door. "Come in!" Ava sang out.

It was too late to answer Ava's question the way it deserved to be answered.

The door was already opening.

Two

Jenna followed the white-haired receptionist along a suspended walkway over a huge open-plan workspace. A wall of glass three stories high highlighted the Seattle cityscape. From there, they turned into a starkly minimalist corridor, paneled with gleaming wood, lit by slanted skylight windows. She'd been wanting to check out the famous new Maddox Hill building in downtown Seattle, made completely out of eco-friendly sustainable wooden building materials, for some time now. Unsurprisingly, it was gorgeous, inside and out. The wood gave it an earthy and welcoming warmth that steel and concrete could never match. A glimpse inside an open office door showed floor-to-ceiling windows and a stunning view of the rapidly transforming city skyline. Just what she'd expect of a world-famous architecture firm.

It was all very elegant, but she wished Ava had kept their original date hours ago at the coffee shop near the Curtis Pavilion, and not strong-armed Jenna into coming up here. She'd hoped for a chance to rehearse the main points of her intro presentation with her friend before she had to give the speech. Ava had a keen ear for anything flat, boring or repetitive.

But whatever. She'd gotten through it okay, even without the dry run, and it was out of her hands now. Fingers and toes crossed. The Wexler Prize was a juicy one. Half a million dollars would kick her research forward and turbocharge all her hopes and plans.

Maybe Ava had just wanted to show off the new Maddox Hill headquarters building, and if so, she was suitably impressed. Her uncle Malcolm Maddox was the firm's cofounder, and the building itself had been recently designed by Ava's sexy brother, Drew, the infamous bad boy of modern architecture.

The receptionist stopped in front of a mahogany door, and knocked.

"Come in!" Ava's voice called.

This room, like the corner office Jenna had glimpsed, was large and featured big slanted windows, and a breath-taking view. The sun glowed low on the horizon, painting the clouds pink. Ava gave her a welcoming smile, and then the man at the table stood up and turned around. Jenna stopped short—and stopped breathing.

Drew Maddox himself, in the flesh. Ava's big brother and architect of the superrich: the tech tycoons, oil sheikhs and Hollywood royalty. Currently the focus of a fresh sex scandal.

And also, incidentally, of her most feverish and long-standing girlish crush. Because of course, she had such impeccable taste in men. Ha ha.

She hadn't seen Drew Maddox since the sangria episode in college. She'd fled the scene in a state of utter mortification, and hadn't come back with a bucket and mop to clean up the mess until he was safely gone. He'd roared off on his motorcycle into the sunset and straight into her wildest sexual fantasies.

Where he proceeded to take up permanent residence. He was her go-to. Always.

He was just as gorgeous now as he ever had been. No, even more so. Eleven years had rendered him denser. More solid and seasoned. Even bigger than she remembered. He was so tall. Broad shouldered, with that tapered waist. Hard muscular thighs. On Drew Maddox, a pair of dress pants, a crisp white shirt and a silk tie looked almost dangerous.

His face was so beautiful. Golden olive skin. Dark hair. Deep-set, tilted green eyes. Lashes longer and darker than any man needed them to be. Sharp cheekbones, a strong, chiseled jaw and full, sensual lips. The dramatic slash of his dark eyebrows was mesmerizing. He was so fine, no wonder women flung themselves at him, at least according to this morning's tabloids. She didn't blame them.

Ava looked discreetly amused when Jenna finally dragged her gaze away.

Damn. Caught gawking. And of course, now her face was red. It was the cross she had to bear, with her pale, redheaded complexion. Freckles and blushing.

"You remember my brother, Drew?" Ava said.

"Of course." Jenna tried to smile. "Our dorm room,

back in college. I believe I dumped a pitcher of sangria all over you."

"I remember that." His voice was so deep and resonant. "It was sticky."

"I was telling Drew about your presentation," Ava said. "I sent him the video Ernest made for me."

Yikes. Fresh insecurity rocked her. Drew, watching her speak? She could have had lipstick on her teeth for all she knew.

"Come in, come in," Ava urged. "Shall I ask Mrs. Crane to bring you coffee, tea, a soft drink? A fresh-pressed juice? We have a juice bar."

"No, thanks. I don't need anything."

"Sit down, Jenna. There's something we needed to ask you."

"Go ahead." Jenna settled herself in a chair, tingling with nerves. Drew stood with his back to them, gazing out the window at the fading sunset colors glowing on the horizon.

Jenna wrenched her gaze away from his perfect, fabulously muscular butt with great force of will. "What is it you want to know?"

"Um… This is kind of awkward." Ava's eyes flicked over to Drew, then back to her. "But we appear to be in some PR trouble. I don't suppose you saw the tabloids today."

"I noticed a couple of silly headlines online this morning," she admitted. "But I didn't read the articles. Nobody pays attention to those rags anyhow."

Total lie. She'd read through all four articles. Every word. In fact, she'd stared avidly at the pictures until her coffee was cold wondering what a guy like Drew

Maddox saw in those pumped-full-of-silicone party girls. Men. She would never understand.

"Triple Towers Starchitect Caught with His Hand in the Cookie Jar!" read one headline. A photo of Drew's Hollywood starlet girlfriend's scowling face was captioned: "Bonita Furious! Bad Boy Drew Maddox strays…again!"

Drew turned around, his mouth grim. "Uncle Malcolm is pissed. But his partner, Hendrick Hill, is the real problem. Hendrick wants me out as CEO on moral grounds. My uncle owns forty percent of the controlling shares, Hendrick has forty, and the other twenty percent are controlled by the rest of the board. With those pictures, Hendrick will be able to persuade over half of them that I'm a liability. And I'll be fired."

"Oh," Jenna murmured, dismayed. "That's terrible. I mean, I'm sure you'll be fine eventually. You're a brilliant architect. Nobody questions your talent. But still. It's awful."

"It is, particularly since those pictures were staged," Ava told her. "He was set up."

Drew made a pained sound. "Ava, do we have to go into the gory details?"

"She needs to know the situation. Be clear. You were lured into that place on false pretenses and ambushed. Those girls jumped on you and posed you for those photographs. We don't know who organized it, but they've gone to a lot of trouble to mess with you, and their plan seems to be working. That's where you come in, Jenna."

"Me?" Jenna looked from Ava to Drew, confused. "How me?"

"Well…we were just thinking—"

"*You* were thinking, Av," Drew said. "Own it."

"Okay, fine. I, Ava Maddox, was thinking, because I am a freaking genius, that a whirlwind engagement would help the optics of the situation. You know, to draw attention away from those pictures. To counter Drew's soulless playboy image."

"Whirlwind engagement with…who?" Jenna's voice trailed off. Heat rushed into her face afresh. "Wait. You can't possibly mean…"

"Yes, exactly! You! Of course you." Her friend's face was bright with enthusiasm. "You're perfect. Smart. Pretty. Respected in your field. You're out there walking the walk, helping people in ways that are concrete and personal. Your social cred would help Drew right now. Plus, Hendrick's a sucker for a romantic story. Uncle Malcolm once told me that Hendrick was quite the naughty bad boy himself, back before he met Bev. He shaped right up when he snagged her. Hendrick and Bev are the real challenge, but I think you could charm them into submission if we moved fast, with assurance. You know, if you guys act as if this were an absolutely done deal, and had been for a while."

Jenna could think of absolutely nothing to say. She forced her mouth to close.

"Of course, we're talking a temporary arrangement," Ava went on. "Just until the fuss blows over and Hendrick calms down. I wouldn't ask if I didn't know for a fact that you're single at the moment."

"Right," she muttered. "No conflicts there at all." Now the heat in her face was in full flower. The humiliation caused by her ex-fiancé Rupert's betrayal was still unpleasantly fresh. Being jilted for Rupert's curvaceous blonde intern had been a nasty blow to her heart and her pride.

"And also, as a bonus… It would not suck to be engaged yourself while that pig-dog Rupert is getting married, right?" Ava pointed out. "Just for a few months."

"Maybe not," Jenna said cautiously. "I guess."

"Be Drew's arm candy," Ava urged. "Attend swanky parties, dressed to kill. Make contacts, rub elbows. This place is crawling with people who have more money than they know how to spend. Teach them to spend it on your research. It's a win-win for everyone. This romance is going to be the magic touch that will shoot the profile of Arm's Reach up into the stratosphere. More than any of my other efforts so far. Brilliant though they are."

Jenna shook her head. "I'm honored to be asked, but I don't think it will work."

"I'd understand if you didn't want your organization associated with this mess," Drew said, gesturing at the pile of tabloids.

"Oh, no," she said hastily. "That's not what I'm saying. Um… The thing is, I just don't think that it would be, you know. Believable. Him and me."

"Why not?" Ava asked. "You two would look adorable together. You'll be the ultimate power couple. Each with his or her own personal superpower."

"Av, get real!" she blurted. "I'm not his type!"

"Type?" Drew frowned at her. "What the hell? What type is that? I don't have a type."

"You are your own individual type, Jenn," Ava soothed. "You're utterly unique. Come on. What do you think? Will you give it a shot? For me?"

"Ah…" Jenna's voice trailed off. "I don't think this makes sense."

"Back off," Drew said sternly to Ava. "You're bull-dozing."

"Of course I am!" Ava protested. "Because I'm right! It would be beneficial to both of you. My spin-doctor instincts are right on the money, every time."

Drew pulled a chair up and sat down near her. So close, she could smell his cologne. A deep, piney, spicy, musky whiff of masculine yum, overwhelming her senses as he gazed searchingly into her face.

He glanced back at Ava. "You really think it will be worth her while? Taking on my bad reputation?"

"Once I get to work on this story? You better believe it'll be worth it." Ava's voice rang with utter conviction. "It'll send her profile through the roof."

Drew turned his gaze back onto Jenna. "I don't like to misrepresent myself," he said. "But if it genuinely makes sense for you, too, I'd be willing to give it a shot."

Make sense for her? She couldn't make sense of a damn thing while she was staring into Drew Maddox's face. *Damn, Jenna. Sharpen up.*

"How about this," Drew went on. "We can give it a trial run tonight. Ava and I were supposed to have dinner with Uncle Malcolm, our cousin Harold, Hendrick and his wife, Beverly. Come with us, just as my date, not my fiancée. We'll see how it feels. See if Hendrick and Bev buy into it. See if it makes you too uncomfortable. If it does, just say no after dinner. No harm, no foul. I will absolutely understand."

"Really? Wouldn't that be, you know...really awkward?"

His smile was so gorgeous. Subtle dimples carved deep into his lean cheeks, bracketing his sexy mouth.

His hypnotically beautiful, long-lashed eyes studied her intently.

"Of course it would be awkward," he said softly. "Welcome to my world."

Ooh. Those words sent inappropriate shivers rushing down her spine.

Drew Maddox waited, eyes fixed on her. After a moment, one of those black winged eyebrows tilted upwards.

She didn't want to imagine the dazzled, starry-eyed look that must be on her face right now.

Just like old times. Ava had dragged her into lots of trouble back in their college days. But this time, it was just playacting, right? In the interests of securing more funding for Arm's Reach. Her cause was a good one. It was worth it.

And what was the harm, really? She wasn't lying to anyone but the predatory gossip rags and this tight-assed partner, Hendrick Hill. And it wasn't a lie that would damage anyone, or take anything from anyone.

Plus, she wasn't locked into it. She could bail tonight if they crashed and burned.

"Okay," Jenna said slowly. "I suppose we could give dinner a try."

Ava's delighted hand-clapping startled Jenna, causing her to sit bolt upright in her chair. "Excellent!" her friend said briskly. "You have just enough time to get home and dress for dinner. You came here in a cab, right?"

"Ah, yes, but—"

"I'll call a car to take you home, and I—hold on a sec." A guitar riff from a classic rock tune came from a smartphone on the table. Ava glanced at the display and tapped the screen, holding it to her ear. "Hey, Ernest. Talk to me…really? Three of them? They're hungry today. Okay, I'll tell them to hurry up. Thanks."

She laid down her phone, her eyes sparkling. "You guys! We have an opportunity to launch this right now with a splash. My assistant, Ernest, has identified three celebrity photographers lurking down in the front lobby, waiting for Drew. Jump on it! Use them for once, instead of letting them use you!"

Jenna drew in a sharp breath. "You mean, paparazzi? They follow you?"

Drew's mouth tightened. "They bother me occasionally, yes."

Ava waved her hand. "Ever since that thing he had with that actress who did the last dinosaur flick, what's her name? Bonita Ramon. It's hard to keep your love affairs straight. Anyhow, the tabloid sharks discovered that stories about Drew sell newspapers even without a movie star attached to him. His money, his looks, his sex life—"

"Ava, don't," he said.

Ava rolled her eyes. "Your own fault for being so damn photogenic. You're, like, walking clickbait. So? They're waiting, people! Go get 'em!"

Ouch. Jenna winced inwardly at the thought of being compared to the radiant movie star, Bonita Ramon. This adventure could prove to be more dangerous to her self-esteem than she'd thought. "You mean, just go downstairs right now? Together?"

"Wait, Av," Drew said. "We told her she could bail after dinner. If she goes out with me now in front of the photographers, she'll be in it up to her neck. No going back."

"So decide now! Call it fate, okay?" Ava pleaded. "Walk through the lobby holding hands. Laugh, smile, flirt, improvise. Seize the day! If this is going to work, you can't be tentative or coy. You have to hit it hard and keep on hitting!"

Drew glanced at her, and shrugged. "Your call, Jenna," he said. "Do not let her pressure you."

Ava clasped pleading hands. "C'mon, Jenn," she coaxed. "Don't you trust me? Tell me you do."

"Hush up and let me think," Jenna said distractedly.

Thinking was hard, with her wits compromised by Drew Maddox's proximity, which created a huge racket in both mind and body.

Drew was right. Going out now nixed any chance of changing her mind discreetly.

Ava was also right. Now was the moment to announce their fake romance to the world. If it was the plan, she should just do it. Waffling and pussyfooting was stupid.

Ava had gotten her into plenty of trouble back in the day, true. On the plus side, most of it had been a blast. The most fun she'd ever had. Before or since.

She looked at Drew, who looked back without smiling, arms crossed over his chest, and her ex-fiancé flashed through her mind. Rupert, who was currently planning his honeymoon with Kayleigh, the twenty-three-year-old intern. She of the big blue eyes that went blinkety-blink like an anime waif. Pouty lips always dangling a little bit open.

The hell with it. Her love life was in a shambles anyway. Empty and sterile and stupid. So why not put it at the service of a friend? Besides, she could use a little goddamn distraction right now. And Arm's Reach needed a good push.

"I'm in," she announced. "Let's go downstairs."

"Yessss!" Ava bounded up to her feet, jubilant. "Go, go, go now! I'll call a car to pick you up out front so they'll have time to get some nice shots of you two together. Don't walk too fast across the lobby. And remember to smile. Oh, and be sure to look up into his—"

"You're micromanaging," Drew said. "Back off. We'll take it from here."

Despite her brother's tone, the irrepressible Ava didn't stop beaming as she herded them down the hall and into one of the elevator banks. She waved excitedly as the doors slid shut.

Suddenly Jenna was alone with Drew Maddox, every angle of his big, stunning self reflected in the gleaming, reflective silver elevator walls, all the way out into infinity.

Whew. That was a whole lot of Drew Maddox to process.

He smelled so good. She was hyperconscious of how well his pants fit. The width of his shoulders. The bulge of his biceps, filling his jacket sleeves, and they weren't even a type of sleeve designed to showcase great biceps.

Say something, Jenna. Speak. "Ah, wow. That was… intense."

"Sure was," he agreed. "Too intense. Ava's classic bulldozer routine. Sorry."

"I'm familiar with it," she told him.

"Yeah? Has she dragged you into her crazy schemes before?"

"All through college," she admitted. "I was a big nerd, trying to squeeze mechanical and electronic engineering into my head, and Ava wanted to save me from myself. It was her sacred mission to get me into a respectable amount of trouble."

He laughed under his breath. "Respectable?"

"Oh, yeah," she assured him. "Only lame-ass losers never get into any trouble."

His teeth flashed, gorgeously white. "Sounds like something Av would say."

"She likes to challenge me," Jenna said. "Get me out of my comfort zone."

"I imagine that's usually a good thing. But seriously. If this makes you uncomfortable, you don't have to do it. No pressure. Are we clear?"

Aw. How sweet. She nodded.

His smile made her legs wobble. "Good. Door's opening. Last chance to bail."

The decision made itself on some deep, wordless level of her mind, just as the doors started to slide open.

She went up onto her tiptoes, cupped the nape of his neck and pulled him down into a forceful kiss.

Drew stiffened for a fraction of an instant—and then leaned into it.

His lips were so warm. She registered the silken texture of his short hair. Touched his cheek with her other hand, exploring the faint, sandpapery rasp of beard shadow, his warm, smooth, supple skin. She was vaguely aware of flashes of light from the cameras, hoots and whistles. They seemed far away. Irrelevant.

Drew swayed back. "Whoa," he murmured. "You took me by surprise."

"Sorry," she whispered back. "Snap decision."

"Don't apologize. I'm there for it. Anytime."

She waited. "So?" she prompted. "Shall we go out there? Get in their faces?"

Drew stuck his hand in the elevator door as it started to close again and they stepped out, shoulder to shoulder, to the constant flashing of the cameras on every side.

Act confident, silly girl. Smile. Act like Drew Maddox is your boyfriend.

Wow, that was some potent make-believe magic. It made her suddenly three inches taller. Her chest swelled out, her chin went up, her face turned pink.

They wound their arms together and clasped hands. Jenna wasn't sure which of them had initiated the contact. It seemed to happen of its own accord. The building security people finally caught up with the photographers and blocked them from following them out the main entrance, and an older man in a suit hurried out after them, his face clearly anxious. "The car's waiting, Mr. Maddox," he said. "I am so sorry about this. We had no idea they were going to descend on you like that."

"It's okay, Mr. Sykes. Let them take all the pictures they want from behind the glass but I'd appreciate if you'd keep them in the lobby until Ms. Somers's car is gone."

Drew pulled her toward the big Mercedes SUV idling at the curb. "Here's your ride," he said. "We still on for tonight? I wouldn't blame you if you changed your mind. The paparazzi are a huge pain in the ass. Like a weather condition. Or a zombie horde."

"I'm still game," she said. "Let 'em do their worst."

That got her a smile that touched off fireworks at every level of her consciousness.

For God's sake. Get a grip, girl.

"I'll pick you up at eight fifteen," he said. "Our reservation at Peccati di Gola is at eight forty-five."

"I'll be ready," she promised.

"Can I put my number into your phone, so you can
text me your address?"

"Of course." She handed him her phone and waited
as he tapped the number into it. He hit Call and waited
for the ring.

"There," she said, taking her phone back. "You've
got me now."

"Lucky me," he murmured. He glanced back at the
photographers, still blocked by three security men at the
door, still snapping photos. "You're no delicate flower,
are you?"

"By no means," she assured him.

"I like that," he said. He'd already opened the car
door for her, but as she was about to get inside, he pulled
her swiftly back up again and covered her mouth with
his.

His kiss was hotter than the last one. Deliberate, demanding. He pressed her closer, tasting her lips.

Oh. Wow. He tasted amazing. Like fire, like wind.
Like sunlight on the ocean. She dug her fingers into
the massive bulk of his shoulders, or tried to. He was
so thick and solid. Her fingers slid helplessly over the
fabric of his jacket. They could get no grip.

His lips parted hers. The tip of his tongue flicked
against hers, coaxed her to open, to give herself up. To
yield to him. His kiss promised infinite pleasure in return. It demanded surrender on a level so deep and pri-
mal, she responded instinctively.

She melted against him with a shudder of emotion
that was absolutely unfaked.

Holy *crap*. Panic pierced her as she realized what was happening. He'd kissed her like he meant it, and she'd responded in the same way. Naturally as breathing.

She was so screwed.

Jenna pulled away, shaking. She felt like a mask had been pulled off. That he could see straight into the depths of her most private self.

Drew helped her into the car and gave her a reassuring smile and a friendly wave as the car pulled away, like it was no big deal. As if he hadn't just tongue-kissed her passionately in front of a crowd of photographers and caused an inner earthquake.

Her lips were still glowing. They tingled from the contact.

She couldn't let her mind stray down this path. She was a means to an end.

It was Drew Maddox's nature to be seductive. He was probably that way with every woman he talked to. He probably couldn't help himself. Not even if he tried.

She had to keep that fact firmly in mind.

All. The. Time.

Three

Drew watched Jenna's recorded online speeches for well over an hour. First the Wexler Prize presentation, then the Women in STEM speech that he found online, then a TED talk she'd done a couple of years ago, then a recent podcast on a popular science show.

He listened to the podcast as he drove home. He liked her clear alto voice. The direct, lucid way that she described her techniques. Her intense enthusiasm and drive. He had friends in the service who'd lost limbs in Iraq and Afghanistan. The implications of her work for them were exciting.

He couldn't wait to get home and watch the video, along with the audio. To see the conviction shining out of her eyes. Her complete, passionate investment in what she was doing.

It was sexy to watch.

He set up the tablet in his bedroom while he was changing for dinner and listened to the TED talk again. He liked the way her voice made him feel. Strange, that he hadn't taken much note of her when they first met. But he'd been a different person back then.

Oddly enough, he'd stopped constantly reliving that fiasco at Arnold Sobel's party since meeting with Jenna. Up until that moment, he'd been seeing it over and over, smelling that foul, drugged perfume that had been sprayed into his face. Remembering the moment he woke up naked in that unfamiliar bed, head throbbing, stomach churning. The bodies of strangers pressed up to him.

He'd been violently sick to his stomach. His head had felt like a mallet slammed into it with each heartbeat. He'd felt humiliated, helpless. And so damn stupid for letting that happen to him.

He hadn't told anyone about the drugged perfume or the blackout. The words stopped in his mouth before they could come out. Humiliation, maybe. Or macho embarrassment. Who knew, but he just couldn't talk about it. Not to anyone.

Meeting Jenna had made that shame evaporate like steam. The surprise kiss in the elevator forced him to drape his coat over his erection. He'd kissed her again at the car just to see if his first reaction was a fluke.

It was not. He'd kept that coat right where it was.

Her kisses were burned into his memory. The feeling of her slim body, molding against him, pliant and trusting. The fine, flower petal texture of her skin. The softness of her lips. Her perfume was a warm, teasing hint of honey, oranges. He'd strained for more of it.

One final detail. He pulled the case that held his

mother's jewelry out of his wall safe. He'd tried to give it to Ava years ago, but she'd burst into tears and run out of the room. So he'd just put the jewelry box away and never mentioned it to her again.

He pulled out the small black velvet box that held Mom's engagement ring. The kiss in front of the gossip rag photographers had committed them to this charade, so the hell with it. He was all in.

With more time to think, he might have gone out and bought a new ring, but Malcolm would recognize Mom's ring, maybe Hendrick, too. Certainly Hendrick's wife would. Bev had been friends with his mother since before he was born. Nothing got past that woman.

Besides, it felt right. Jenna was the kind of woman to whom a guy would give his mother's engagement ring. Mom would have liked Jenna.

He put his coat on and stuck the ring in his pocket and headed for the car. Thinking about Mom and her ring had triggered an uncomfortable line of thought.

Namely, that Mom would not have approved of him using Jenna like this. Taking advantage of her hard-won assets for his own agenda.

Using her to clean up his mess, essentially.

That uneasy thought tugged on his mind. He tried to rationalize it in every way he could. He had not gotten into this trouble because of his own depraved behavior. He'd been trying to help a friend. The only thing he was guilty of was being stupid, and not jumping clear before the trap closed. His conscience was clear.

Besides, Jenna had her own fish to fry. This situation was in both of their best interests. No one had been fooled. No one was being coerced. It was completely mutual.

The accident that killed his parents was eighteen long years ago, and yet he could still see so clearly that look Mom gave him when he was less than truthful, or when she'd caught him taking a lazy shortcut. Her tight mouth. The frown between her eyes.

In spite of Mom's disapproving look in his mind's eye, the closer he got to Jenna's place in Greenwood, the more buzzed he felt. He was actually looking forward to this. He couldn't even remember the last time he'd felt that way.

Drew parked on the steep slope in front of an attractive three-story house. Jenna's apartment was on the top floor. An external staircase led him up to a comfortable wraparound deck furnished with a swing and wicker furniture. He buzzed her doorbell.

It opened after a moment, and Jenna smiled up at him. "Right on time, I see," she said. "I like that in a man. Come on in."

He couldn't think of anything to say for a moment. Sensory overload shorted him out. Her figure-hugging, textured, forest green dress looked amazing. It accentuated her high, full breasts, nipped-in waist and luscious round bottom, and the color was great for her flame-bright hair, which was twisted into an updo like a fiery halo.

Cat-eye glasses again. Amber-tinted tortoiseshell, with glittery stones in their pointy tips, which matched her drop earrings, but her huge smile outshone it all. Ruby-red lipstick. Beautiful white teeth. A gray cat leaped over his feet and darted out the door.

"You look great," he offered. "I like the glitter on your glasses. Hey, your cat just ran outside. Is that a problem?"

She beckoned him in. "Not at all. He has his own cat door. Plus, he wants dinner, so he'll be back soon. My rhinestone-studded specs only come out for the special occasions, by the way. If the paparazzi show up, I'll blind them with my bling."

"Perfect." He pulled the ring box out. "Speaking of bling, I brought this, if you feel comfortable wearing it. Since you really went for it this afternoon in the lobby."

He opened the box. Jenna blinked, taken aback. "Oh, my gosh. Is that real?"

"Teardrop sapphire with diamond baguettes. It belonged to my mother."

Jenna's eyes went wide and somber behind her glasses. "Um… Are you sure? I mean, since this isn't a real thing, maybe we shouldn't…"

"Malcolm, Hendrick and Bev will all recognize this ring," he told her.

"Oh. Well. In that case, I suppose it makes sense." There was a tiny frown line between her dark eyebrows as he took it out and slid it onto her ring finger.

It fit perfectly. Her cheeks flushed, and her gaze dropped. "It's beautiful," she murmured. "I'll be careful. I know how precious it is."

On impulse, he lifted her hand to his lips and kissed it.

Jenna froze, the color in her cheeks deepening, and tugged her hand free. "Excuse me. Gotta, um, feed my cat. Before we, um, go." She hurried into the kitchen.

Drew wandered around the open-plan apartment. A sliding picture window opened out onto the deck overlooking the backyard. City lights twinkled below it. The living room was separated by a bar from the kitchen, and a couch and a cushy armchair were angled around a TV. The rest of the room was dominated by a long worktable, lit up by industrial hanging lamps and piled with cables, electronic components and schematics. The walls were paneled with corkboard, and a mosaic of information was attached, as well as dozens of photographs. Jenna with various other people. One was a child with a gap-toothed grin, holding up two prosthetic arms triumphantly high in a double thumbs-up.

Jenna came back into the room buttoning up a long, nipped-in black wool coat.

"Is this where you do your research?" he asked her.

"Most of it I do at the Arm's Reach lab. But I like having a workspace at home. When I get ideas, I like to have everything I need to pin them down fast."

He strolled around, gazing at the schematics tacked to the wall. "Impressive."

"So is the Triple Towers sustainable housing complex in Tokyo," she said. "That's some truly amazing, forward-thinking design. Congratulations for your prize, by the way."

"You heard about that?"

"Read about it online. *Time* magazine, I think. Great profile they wrote about you, too. Fawning, even."

"Was it? I didn't notice."

She smiled at him. There was a moment of odd silence, and Jenna gestured toward the door. "Smudge can let himself in the cat door whenever he's ready for his dinner, so shall we go? I wouldn't want to be late."

"Right."

Drew got her settled into his car before getting inside himself. As he turned the key in the ignition, the podcast he'd been listening to on the drive over blared out of the speakers, startlingly loud without the car noise to cover them.

"...*with artificial sensory nerves, the issues are different,*" recorded Jenna said to the podcaster. "*We've brought together many different lines of research in the—*"

He switched it off. Damn. That podcast was online, out in the public domain, and yet still he felt as if he'd been caught snooping in her phone.

"Holy cow," Jenna said, startled. "Was that me? The *Outside the Box* podcast?"

"Yeah. Just, you know. Informing myself about who you are. What you do."

"Oh, of course," she said quickly. "That makes sense. I should have done the same. But I probably know more about your business just because Ava keeps me up to date on the big stuff. Prizes, and all that. She's so proud of you. She boasts and gloats nonstop."

They drove in silence for a while, and finally Drew found the nerve to say it. "I saw your Women in STEM talk, too. The TED talk. And your Wexler Prize presentation speech."

She gave him a startled glance. "Good Lord. All that tonight?"

"You're an excellent speaker," he said. "I got sucked in. Didn't want to stop."

Her eyes slid away, but she looked pleased. "It was hard-won," she admitted. "Public speaking terrified me for the longest time. But I just kept at it until I could power through. I can't believe you watched all that stuff in one go."

"It was fascinating," he said. "Clear, convincing, well structured. Funny."

"Oh. Well. Thanks, that's, ah…encouraging." Jenna twisted her hands together, wrapping the strap of her purse around them. Twirling the engagement ring.

"You don't need to be nervous tonight," he said.

She let out an ironic snort. "Are you kidding? How can I not be?"

"After watching those speeches, I think you'll be great."

"At what? Presenting myself as something I'm not?"

"That's not what you're doing. You just need to be yourself. That's why we asked you to do this."

"Oh, yeah. Just act like a woman who's gotten herself engaged to a guy like you. No biggie." She laughed under her breath. "The more I think about it, the less credible it seems."

"Why?" Drew was genuinely baffled. "What do you mean by a guy like me?"

"Please," she scoffed. "Give me a break. You're a world-renowned architect. You run in exalted social circles. You're American royalty. You went out with Bonita Ramon, for God's sake, and then for your next relationship, you hook up with me? Jenna Somers, Super-Nerd? Anything sound weird about that?"

"I don't see anything," he said. "What does Bonita have to do with it? That's over." Not that it ever really began.

Jenna snorted. "If you have to ask, I don't know how to begin to explain it to you."

Drew blew out a frustrated breath. "I met Bonita at a yacht party in Greece. She was on the rebound from some asshat producer. We hung out for a couple of days, and found out fast that we didn't have much to talk about."

Bonita was also a self-absorbed whiner with a huge personality disorder, and she'd bored him practically into a coma by the end of the second day, but he would never say that to anyone. Kissing-and-telling was for losers with no self-discipline or class.

"Wow," she said. "So. Do you often party with movie stars on yachts in Greece?"

He felt defensive. "I was in Crete for work. I got a call from some friends who were vacationing there. I'm not a coked-out party animal stumbling from orgy to orgy."

"Not at all," she soothed. "I didn't mean to offend you."

"No offense taken. But after the past few days…aw, hell. Sorry to bark at you."

"Don't mention it," she said. "Relax. We'll just play our parts and hope for the best. Can't ask for more than that."

He pulled to a stop in front of the hotel that housed the restaurant and got out, giving his keys to the parking attendant. Jenna got out herself before he had a chance to open the door for her. He took her arm, and the light weight of it felt good. Mom's ring glittered on her slender, capable-looking hand. It looked like she'd been born to wear it.

Out of nowhere, he felt irrationally angry. It was humiliating that he had to hustle and con and play games to protect his professional position. To beg and plead for the help of a woman like Jenna to lend him some goddamn credibility, instead of being taken seriously by her. Courting her with class. Blowing her mind properly.

Jenna must have felt his frustration, sensitive as she was, because she shot him a troubled glance. He manufactured a reassuring smile, but she didn't look convinced.

Jenna was playing along with this scheme out of loyalty to Ava. She was sorry for her friend's screwup brother. That poor sorry bastard who couldn't keep his act together.

Play our parts and hope for the best. Can't ask for more than that, she'd said.

Like hell. He did want more than that. He didn't want to make do with crumbs.

He wanted it all, whether he deserved it or not.

Four

Jenna shook hands and smiled until her cheeks ached as Ava and Drew introduced her to the people at the table in the restaurant. Ava looked gorgeous in her skin-tight black lace dress. Ava and Drew's cousin Harold Maddox was there, straitlaced and unsmiling in his dark suit and tie. Harold had the Maddox height and good looks, but he wasn't as striking as Drew and Ava. Drew's Uncle Malcolm she'd already seen in Ava's pictures. He was an older, grimmer version of Drew, shriveled by age and twisted by arthritis. Malcolm's partner, Hendrick Hill, was bone-thin and bald, with sharp cheekbones and sunken cheeks. He studied her doubtfully with deep-set, suspicious eyes beneath thick black-beetled brows. His wife, Beverly, was his polar opposite. Short, round and friendly, she had a blindingly white pixie cut and lots of white gold jewelry dangling over her midnight-blue silk caftan. Her smile froze for only a moment when Drew introduced her as his fiancée, and all eyes fastened instantly on Jenna's hand, which she'd been quick to position so that the stunning engagement ring was visible to all.

"Fiancée?" Malcolm Maddox's bushy gray brows knit together. "What's this? How is it that I've never laid eyes on you before? Where did you come from, girl?"

"Uncle," Ava reproved him. "Manners, please. She's an old friend of mine, and you're meeting her now. Be nice."

"I was just waiting for the right moment to tell you, Uncle," Drew said. "Things got crazy."

"Hmmph," Harold muttered. "I'll just bet they did."

Ava elbowed Harold, but no one else seemed to notice. They were all staring at her. Then Bev's brilliant smile flashed as she made her way around the table to hug and kiss Jenna. "Oh, my goodness! Congratulations! How exciting. I wish you all the best."

The warmth of the older woman's good wishes made Jenna feel guilty. The benevolent older lady reminded her of her own mother, gone six years now.

The meal proceeded pleasantly enough. Jenna had Drew on one side and Bev on the other, and Ava and Bev were both masters of the art of cheerful, entertaining chitchat, to which Jenna did her best to contribute, though it was hard to concentrate with a scowling Uncle Malcolm dissecting her furiously with his eyes from across the table.

Sometime after the appetizers, Bev took her hand and lifted it to examine the sapphire ring. "The sight of that ring really brings me back," she murmured, a catch in her voice. "Diana and I were sorority sisters, back in the day. She was so special. Brilliant, funny. A real beauty. Ava is her living image. I miss her so much, even now."

Jenna smiled into the wet eyes of the other woman, and squeezed her hand. "I wish I could have known her."

"Oh, me, too." Bev dabbed at her eyes with a tissue, sniffing delicately. "So, how did you and Drew meet, anyway?"

Jenna froze, panicked, and Ava piped up. "Oh, that was my doing. I take full credit for that. I am Cupid personified, people. Arrows and all."

"Why am I not surprised," Uncle Malcolm muttered.

"I met him for the first time eleven years ago," Jenna explained. "Back when Ava and I were in college."

"I was on leave," Drew said. "In between tours in Iraq."

"He came to visit me on his way to Canada," Ava said. "He was going to do the Banff-Jasper Highway in the Canadian Rockies on his motorcycle."

"So long ago?" Bev looked bewildered.

"That was long before we got together," Jenna explained. "He was unimpressed with me at the time, particularly after I dumped a pitcher of sangria all over him. Not my finest moment."

"Oh, dear." Bev tittered into her white wine. "How awful."

"It was," Jenna said ruefully. "I wanted to die."

"I'm glad you didn't." Drew lifted her other hand to his lips and pressed a hot, seductive kiss against her fingers that sent shivers rippling through her body. "My shoes stuck to the floor when I walked for days afterward. But it was worth it in the end. Baptized by Gallo port and peach nectar."

His smile made her go molten inside. Oh, he was good. She knew it was for show, and even so it made her feel like she was the only woman in the world. And now she was staring back at him, starry-eyed, mouth slightly open, having completely lost her train of thought. The Drew effect. Whoa. Debilitating.

The waiter arrived and began serving the entrees. Bev patted her hand and waited, clearly amused, while Jenna struggled to orient herself in the conversation.

"So, when did you and Drew reconnect?" Bev asked, gently nudging her back on track.

Another split-second-panicked pause, and once again Ava jumped to the rescue.

"Actually, that was my fault, too," Ava said. "Last spring Jenna asked me to do PR for her Arm's Reach Foundation, so I went down to see the Women in STEM speech in San Francisco to talk strategy. Drew was down there, too, working on the Magnolia Plaza job. The three of us had dinner, and it all came together. Like magic."

Jenna stabbed a couple of penne with vodka sauce on the end of her fork, trying to breathe down the panic. Okay. Thanks to Ava, she and Drew now had an origin story. Yay.

Drew's eyebrow tilted up for an instant, like Ava's did when she was doubtful about something. Then he kissed her hand, going with it. "Changed my life," he murmured.

"Huh. I was down in San Francisco working on Magnolia Plaza, too," Harold said slowly. "Funny that

I never ran into Jenna once that entire time. We were there for three months."

Ava shrugged. "Doesn't seem funny to me," she said. "You weren't with us on those nights."

"Evidently," Harold said. "But I did not get the impression that Drew was engaged to anyone during that time." He gave Drew a thin, knowing smile. "On the contrary."

"Women in STEM, did you say?" Bev swooped in to salvage the conversation, sensing tension in the air. "What was it Ava said you did, dear? Some sort of engineer, right?"

"Yes. I design neuro-prosthetic devices," Jenna explained.

Bev blinked. "Ah. I see."

"She designs brain-directed bionic limbs for amputees that give actual sensory feedback," Drew broke in. "It's overly modest to just say, 'I design neuro-prosthetic devices.'"

Jenna laid down her fork. "I didn't think this was the time or place," she told him sternly. "But I do know how to toot my own horn."

"Yes, but this actually is the time and place," Drew said. "Bev works with the Bricker Foundation, so she needs to know about Arm's Reach." He looked at Bev. "I'll send you the link to the Women in STEM speech. You'll be intrigued, considering your work with veterans."

Bev sipped her wine, her eyes sparkling behind her rimless glasses. "Thank you, Drew. By all means, do send me that link."

"The TED talk is fine for a quick overview," Drew

went on. "But the Women in STEM speech goes into much more detail."

"And there's the Wexler Prize presentation she gave today at the Curtis." Ava picked up her phone and tapped it. "Forwarding video links right now, Bev."

"I can't wait to see them." Bev smiled, her eyes soft. "I love how he's so proud of you. That's just as it should be."

Another awkward pause. Everyone's eyes on her. She was starting to sweat.

"You certainly have been doing your homework, Drew," Uncle Malcolm said.

"Just admiring my fiancée's accomplishments," Drew said. "It's worth a look. She does groundbreaking work that transforms people's lives."

Malcolm grumbled under his breath. "I'm sure it does. Yours included, eh? So she just pops out of the woodwork, fully formed and already engaged to you?" He scowled in Ava's direction. "You plotting and scheming again, girl? I know your tricks."

Ava batted her big gray eyes at him. "Uncle," she murmured. "You wound me."

"Ha," Malcolm grunted. "Suffer."

Hoo-boy. Jenna did not want to hear them thrash this one out right in front of her. Time out. She jumped to her feet. "Excuse me, everyone. Back in a moment."

She fled toward the ladies' room, grateful for some air and a break from all that intense scrutiny. To say nothing of the mind-jamming effect of Drew's over-the-top hotness. She lingered in one of the stalls, trying to settle herself with deep, slow breaths.

This was trickier than she'd anticipated. She disliked lying on principle, and hated lying to people she liked. And she liked Bev Hill. Hendrick still had that mistrustful pucker to his mouth, and Malcolm Maddox couldn't stop frowning. Both men were hyper-wary of a trap, but not Bev. She was sweet and warm and genuine.

Jenna came out, straightened herself up, washed her hands at the gray marble sink and tried, more or less in vain, to get her hair in order. She was touching up her mascara when Bev came out of one of the bathroom stalls. Bev waited for another couple of women who were there to finish their washing and primping and walk out.

As soon as they did, Bev moved closer and placed her hand on Jenna's shoulder.

"Honey. I have to say something to you," she said earnestly. "I don't have the right to say this yet, since we just met. But you seem like a lovely girl, so I'm going to risk it."

Jenna braced herself. "What is it?"

Bev's eyes were anxious. "How well do you really know Drew Maddox? I mean, beyond the sangria and the meeting in San Francisco. Do you really know him?"

"Ah… I, um…" Jenna stammered, groping for words. "Bev…"

"I know I just met you, and have no right to ask," Bev said swiftly. "And it was clear to everyone that you're madly in love with him, so I'm sorry to cause you any pain."

Jenna tried not to wince. So her crush was really that visible. "Bev, um… I just—"

"He's ridiculously handsome, yes. Far more so than is healthy for him. Brilliant, talented, charming. Naturally seductive. Ava, too. Their parents both were, and

Malcolm was, too, back in the day. But Jenna... I don't know how to say this, but—"

"You don't have to," Jenna said. "I know Drew didn't live like a monk before we got together. His love life would be hard not to notice even if you wanted to ignore it."

"Well, thank goodness you're aware of that. But I... I just wanted you to be forewarned of, ah..." Her voice trailed off. She looked pained.

"I assume you're referring to the pictures in the tabloids lately?"

Bev's lips tightened. "I'm glad you know about them. I would hate to be the one to tell you."

"It's not what it seems," Jenna explained. "Drew got ambushed by the photographer and the girls when he got to that party. The whole thing was staged."

"Oh." Bev's lips were still compressed. "Is that a fact?"

"It is," Jenna insisted. "Really. Someone is trying to take him down."

"You truly believe that?"

"One hundred percent," Jenna said firmly. "Not a doubt in my mind."

Bev let out a sharp little sigh. "Well, then. If you're sure, then I suppose there's nothing left to say, honey. Except sorry, for overstepping my bounds."

"I know it came from a good place," Jenna said. "You're very kind. Trying to protect me when you barely even know me."

"That's a generous way for you to look at it, my dear," Bev said. "My husband and I were worried the second he introduced you as his fiancée. We just hate to see a lovely young woman with all that energy and promise running right off a cliff."

"No cliffs, I promise," she assured the other woman. "My heart is safe."

"Good luck with that, honey." Bev patted her shoulder with a smile. "But it's not supposed to be safe, you know. That's not what hearts are for."

Five

Drew gazed after Jenna as she vanished around the corner on her way to the bathroom. Bev got up and excused herself shortly afterward to follow her. Then Hendrick mumbled some inaudible excuse and fled, which surprised no one. Hendrick could tolerate mixed social situations only if Bev was by his side.

That left Ava, his cousin and Uncle Malcolm. All family. No one left at the table to constrain his uncle to basic politeness. He'd been tossed to the wolves.

Uncle Malcolm got to it without losing time, wiping his mouth aggressively with a napkin. "So, then," he growled. "Jenna Somers, eh? Quick and well-timed, wasn't it? Engaged to a scientist philanthropist, out of the blue? She's not your usual type, boy."

"I don't have a type," Drew said.

"I told you," Ava butted in. "Jenna was my college roommate. She's my best friend in the world, and she—"

"I'm not talking to you, girl. I'm talking to your brother. Why don't you run along and powder your nose with the other females?"

Ava's eyes flashed. "I don't need to pee, Uncle," she said through her teeth. "And I don't run from a fight, either. Guess who taught me not to?"

Uncle Malcolm made an impatient sound. "I don't want to fight with you, girl. I want to talk to him." He jerked his chin toward Drew. "Privately."

"Tough," Ava said. "You want privacy, make a private appointment in your office. Don't banish me from the table at a public restaurant during a dinner party. That's just rude. Jenna is perfect. There is no way that you could object to—"

"Too perfect," Malcolm said grimly. "You don't pull a woman like that out of a hat. You two are cooking up some scheme, and I want to know what's up."

"Nothing is up," Ava said. "No schemes. Just true love. What's the harm?"

"Probably none, for Drew." Harold sounded smug.

"Exactly," Uncle Malcolm said. "The harm will all be to her when she realizes that she's been sold a bill of goods. No nice young lady deserves that."

Drew stared his uncle down. "Thanks for the vote of confidence," he said.

"I'll have confidence in you when you earn it," was Malcolm's curt reply.

At that moment, Jenna and Bev reappeared, engaged in a lively conversation about Jenna's company. Hendrick trailed close behind.

"…to widen my reach," Jenna was saying as the two

of them drew nearer. "I would love to meet with them. It sounds like we would be a perfect fit."

"Wonderful," Bev said briskly. "I'll get back to you first thing tomorrow about possible times, as soon as I speak to Jayne and Helen and take a look at their schedules."

"Don't forget that we'll be busy all day tomorrow," Ava reminded her. "My whole crew, along with Drew, are going to be at Arm's Reach, filming a new install-ment of our video series."

"Me?" Drew said, startled.

"Of course you," Ava said. "Eight thirty on the dot. Ruby's Café is the rendezvous point, on Hatton Street, just a couple of blocks from Jenna's house. My camera crew will meet us there, we'll all grab some breakfast, and off we go to shoot our video."

"What exactly are we shooting? And how long will it take?"

"You'll see," Ava said airily. "Jenna will show us all how the prosthetics function. It'll be fascinating. Don't worry, you can go back to your crazy fourteen-hour workday soon enough. I already talked to both of your assistants. They're on board."

"I can manage my own damn staff, Ava."

She smiled at him, all sweetness. "Just trying to help."

Coffee and dessert arrived, as if Ava had timed it herself, and for a while they were all taken up with sampling tiramisu, panna cotta and the pine-nut cream pastry. Hendrick and Bev said their goodbyes, and Bev gave Jenna a hug, murmuring something into her ear that made Jenna laugh.

Uncle Malcolm shrugged on his coat and made a

point of limping around the table and taking Jenna's hand, frowning into her eyes. "I hope you know what you're doing, young lady. You look like a fine girl, but I believe you're in over your head with this one."

"We'll see about that." She leaned close to kiss his leathery cheek. "Don't underestimate me, Mr. Maddox," she murmured. "Or him."

"Hmmph," he muttered. For a fleeting moment, it almost looked as if he were threatening to smile. "Good night. Harold, my cane. See me down to the car, please."

Harold took Uncle Malcolm by the arm, and Drew, Ava and Jenna all watched their cousin help Malcolm down the staircase.

When they were out the door, Ava threw herself at Jenna and hugged her. "Jenna, you were brilliant. They were eating out of your hand. I would never have guessed that you two weren't wildly in love. Bev was charmed to pieces, and Hendrick will follow anywhere Bev leads. Like a lap dog."

Jenna pulled away, looking flustered. "She is a lovely person."

"And so are you! Like recognizes like!" Ava swatted her brother on the chest. "And that bit about her work, how she was underselling it? Genius, bro. Simply inspired."

His sister's words irritated him, obscurely. "I wasn't acting at all. It's just stating the truth as I saw it."

"Right!" Ava crowed. "Perfect! My plan is working. Don't deny it!"

"We're not denying anything," Jenna said. "It's just complicated. It's doesn't feel good, to tell a lie to a person like Bev."

Ava gazed at Jenna with a puzzled frown. "I suppose

it's not ideal," she admitted. "But desperate times, desperate measures, right?"

"Let it go, Av," Drew said. "It's been a long day. We're tired, and you're bulldozing again."

Ava took a step back, laughing. "Well, now. Look at the two of you, defending each other. In cahoots against me. That is freaking adorable."

"Av, don't condescend," Jenna said wearily.

Ava backed away. "Okay, okay. See you two lovebirds bright and early at Ruby's. Night!"

Drew and Jenna stood there after Ava disappeared, locked in an embarrassed silence.

"So did Bev corner you in the ladies' room?" he finally asked. "When she excused herself she had the look of a woman on a divine mission."

"She was worried about me," Jenna admitted. "Poor innocent maiden that I am, falling prey to a heartless seducer's honeyed promises."

Drew winced. "I'm sorry she feels that way about me."

"I told her you were set up. I'm not sure if she bought it, but she feels sorry for me, and she believes that I believe. I guess our performance was, um…convincing." Her eyes slid away. Her face was pink.

"I guess it was." Drew waited for a cue, but she wouldn't meet his eyes, so he had to just throw his invite out there into the cold with no clue how she'd receive it.

"Want to go somewhere else?" he asked her. "We could get a drink. Hash it out."

She looked up and finally gave him what he'd been craving. That nerve-jolting rush from eye contact. Her big hazel eyes. Streaks of green and gold and a border of dark slate, setting all the bright inner colors off.

She caught her full red lower lip between her teeth, her delicate blush deepening. "Actually, it's been a long, weird day, and tomorrow will be another one. We'd better catch some sleep, if we're going to meet up with Ava's crew at eight thirty."

He let out a silent sigh, crestfallen. "Okay. I'll just take you home."

"Oh, no. I can call a car. There's no need for you to—"

"I insist," he said.

There was a brief struggle, but he managed to persuade her. Once she was inside his car, the self-conscious silence between them deepened. He kept sneaking quick glances, catching the curve of her high cheekbone, the glitter on her glasses. The flash of the ring on her finger. He felt as nervous as an adolescent, asking a girl on a date for the first time. Tongue-tied and struggling.

"Usually Ava drives me crazy when she lets her mouth run," he said. "But she saved the day with that dinner–in–San Francisco story. It should have occurred to me to get our stories straight on the ride over here, but I didn't even think of it."

"I forgot, too," Jenna said. "Thank God Ava thinks on her feet. I'm not much of an improviser. There was no time to think it all through."

"Sorry about that," he said. "We rushed you into this."

"It's okay," she assured him. "I agreed to this freely. No one coerced me."

He pulled up in front of her apartment and killed the engine. "Good. I'm glad you met Bev. She's a good person for you to know. She's connected and extremely committed to her charitable enterprises at the Bricker Foundation. I want this arrangement to be useful for you."

"I'm sure it will be." She smiled at him. "Good night, Drew. Thanks for the ride."

"Let me walk you to your door."

"Oh, no. That's not necessary—"

"Please. I'd prefer to see you safely inside."

Jenna sighed. "Fine. If you insist."

Drew followed her up the stairway and stood at the end of the porch, waiting while she dug in her purse.

"I don't usually fumble for the key, I'll have you know," she told him. "Normally, I'd have it in my hand, ready to jab into an assailant's eyes. I'm a little off my game tonight."

She opened the door, and looked up, opening her mouth to say goodbye, and wild energy suddenly arced between them. The breathless silence felt charged with meaning. Possibility.

Jenna held the door open and shifted back, making room for him to come inside.

She closed the door after he followed her, hung her key ring on the hook on the wall, placed her purse on the shelf and stood there waiting. Seconds passed. They turned into minutes.

"Is there something you wanted to say to me?" Jenna's voice was a soft, throaty whisper.

Yes. But not in words. Words had abandoned him. Something else had taken him over. Something hungry, restless, prowling.

Jenna made a startled sound as he reached out and took her glasses off. He placed them on the shelf by the door, his movements slow and deliberate.

Her hands floated up, but not to push his hands away. He touched her jaw, her cheekbones, with his fingertips. The tender skin at the nape of her neck, behind her ear. The warmth of her hands came to rest on top of his, brushing along his fingers, then pressing his hands against her face.

Every part of her was just as soft and fragrant as he remembered from that astonishing kiss outside the Maddox Hill building.

Her arms wound around his neck. He cupped the back of her head, the thick mass of twisted curls wound up in the back, the ringlets coming loose and twining around his fingers. Breathing in her perfume.

Scolding voices in his head yapped at him. He shouldn't be doing this. It was irresponsible. He was being a self-serving tool. This was going to blow up in his face, and there would be no one to blame but himself.

The voices faded to a background buzz. Distant, irrelevant. And then he was kissing her.

Wildly, like he was starving for her.

Six

It was happening again. He'd bypassed her brain. Just reached past it into something deeper, rawer, truer. A part that didn't care about consequences. It just wanted more of that delicious, virile, wonderful-smelling man who was ravishing her mouth with slow, enthralling skill. *More.*

He lifted her up, and she just clung, like he was her center of gravity, winding her legs around him. He pressed her against the door, letting the hard, unyielding bulge of his erection rock against that tender ache of need between her legs as he kissed her, making her shift and move and moan. She held him tighter, moving over him until he was positioned right where she needed him to be, and then moving again…squeezing. Even through all those layers of cloth, his natural, innate skill was electric, amazing. The way he touched her, as if his hands just sank magically inside her senses, stroking her, changing her. Transforming her.

Jenna pulled him closer, having forgotten completely to be embarrassed about it. He was pulling the stretchy fabric of her bodice down over the low-cut cups of her bra, and she helped him do it, arching her back and holding his head against her chest. His lips felt amazing. Now he was caressing her breasts, circling her nipples through the lace of her bra. Every slow, deliberate caress a delicious lick of flame that sent shivers of anticipation through her body, jacking up the sensations to exquisite madness. She writhed against him, rocking, holding tighter—

And exploded, into pure bliss. Endless pulsing waves of it rushing through her. Sweet, pure, blinding pleasure beyond anything she'd ever felt. Or even imagined.

She came back to herself slowly, feeling so limp and soft, she could barely breathe. She was still pressed to the door, pinned by his body. Her face rested against his big, broad shoulder. Her legs were still wound around his.

She lifted her head. Her face was burning. Good thing his coat was dark, because her eyes were wet, and her mascara was in a highly unstable state.

Drew nuzzled her ear, kissing her throat. Slow, soothing, seductive kisses that promised more, more, more. As much as she could take. For as long as she wanted. His erection still pressed against her, since she was practically astride it. But he wasn't moving or pushing. He was still, waiting for a cue from her.

It took a few panting, shivering minutes to work up the courage to look into his eyes, as reality began to grip her mind again. The hard truth behind this craziness.

This could not happen. Being dumped by Rupert had already left her heart bruised. This was just a game Drew was playing. There was no way it could end up someplace real. She couldn't do this to herself.

She just…didn't…dare.

"Wow," she whispered, licking her trembling lips. "Where did that come from?"

"Let's find out." His voice was a velvety rasp, stroking all her secret senses. "Let's explore it. See how far it goes. How deep. Just say the word."

Before she could stop herself, her mind began to whirl with images of Drew Maddox, naked in her bed. She'd imagined him there often enough. He'd starred in her sexual fantasies ever since she first laid eyes on him.

But Drew always kept it superlight when it came to sex. He was famous for it, while she herself had never been very good at not caring too much when things got intimate. She certainly wouldn't be able to pull it off with a guy she'd had a massive, blazing crush on for over a decade.

Jenna knew how this would go. He'd amuse himself with her, and he'd be great in bed. It would be mind-blowing. Delicious. He would rock her world. Best sex ever.

Then boom, she'd fall for him like a ton of broken rock. He'd be embarrassed by her intensity and pull back fast. She'd be humiliated and hurt, hating herself for being so stupid when she knew the outcome from the start. Why even begin that sad story?

No. She was not going to hurt herself like that. No matter how tempting he was.

She steeled herself. "I think, um…that we've had a miscommunication," she said carefully. "I'm really sorry, but when I agreed to this, I never meant to put sex on the table as part of the bargain. That's just not who I am."

Tension gripped him. He shifted back, and she slid down his legs as he set her gently on her feet. "I never dreamed that you were," he said.

Jenna fumbled with the neckline of her dress, trying to get it up over the cups of her bra. "I'm sorry if I sent mixed messages. Made things more complicated."

"Complicated why? Because I made you come? Don't worry about it. You're so beautiful. It was incredible to watch. I'll dream about it all night long."

"Oh, stop that," she said sharply.

He looked startled. "Stop what?"

"The smooth lover-boy routine that makes all the ladies melt." She backed away from him. "I don't want to join the Drew Maddox fan club. I'd get lost in the crowd."

His face didn't change expression, but she saw startled hurt in his eyes.

"I apologize," he said. "I misread your cues. I'll get out of your way now."

The look on his face made her feel terrible. His only crime was in kissing and caressing her into a fabulous orgasm, and here she was, punishing him for it.

"Damn it, Drew," she said miserably. "I'm sorry. I didn't mean—"

"Excuse me." Drew nudged her to the side. "Scoot over, please. I need to get through the door."

He pulled it open. Jenna followed him out onto the porch. "Look, what I said was unfair," she called after him. "I wish I hadn't said it."

Drew lifted his hand without turning. "Don't sweat it. I appreciate that you're honest. Good night, Jenna."

She watched from the top of the stairs as he got into his car. The lights flicked on, the engine purred to life, and she dug her fingernails into the wooden porch railing, resisting the urge to run down the stairs after him, waving her arms.

Come back. Give me some more of that. I didn't mean it. I'm sorry. Forgive me.

She clamped down on the impulse. Her track record with men so far was spotty, Rupert being her latest disaster. She'd let him use her to further his own career and found herself ignominiously dumped, three months before their planned wedding date.

Odd how it had felt like such a huge disaster at the time, but at the moment, she could hardly remember now how she'd felt about it. All the hurt, mortification and embarrassment had been completely eclipsed by what she was feeling right now. After just a few kisses.

It hurt so badly, to shut Drew out. Like she'd just killed something beautiful and magical, full of unknown, shining possibilities.

But she had to do it. Because it was a trap, damn it. A pretty illusion. She had to be realistic. Drew Maddox would fulfill all her wildest dreams while he was giving her his undivided attention...until suddenly, when she least expected it, and for whatever reason, he no longer did.

At which point, she'd fall right off the edge of the world.

The night was so damn long when he couldn't sleep, which was often. He'd suffered from stress flashbacks for years after his deployment. Even now his sleep was often troubled and fractured by nightmares.

Drew came to a decision in the interminable darkness, as he stared at his bedroom ceiling. It sucked, to be awake in the darkest, deepest part of the night. Stiff as a board, mind racing with every shortcoming, every screwup, every wrong move he'd ever made.

This mess being the latest, and greatest, of many. He'd been insane to let Ava drag him into this. But if he was honest with himself, he had to admit that he'd done it because he was intrigued by Jenna herself. He'd wanted to get closer.

Now her words kept echoing in his head. *Stop the smooth lover-boy routine. I don't want to join the Drew Maddox fan club. I'd get lost in the crowd.*

Lost in the goddamn *crowd*? Seriously?

Man slut. Playboy. User. That was his rep now? Would that be his legacy?

Not all of it was deserved. Only a tiny percentage. He'd had a few talkative, angry drama-queen ex-lovers. After Bonita, he'd attracted the attention of the tabloid press, and this was the result. His current nightmare, Sobel's party being the crowning disaster.

The thought of that night made his gut clench. He was a decorated Marine, and a hundred-and-ten-pound showgirl with glitter on her eyelashes had taken him down with a drugged perfume bottle. It made him sick.

The best trick to beat that nausea was to think about Jenna. Her softness, her scent, her incendiary kisses, her gorgeous eyes. But that was a pitfall now.

He shouldn't have come on to her but something huge and ruthless had reached inside and grabbed hold of him. Made him do and say things that were head-up-ass stupid.

Screw this. He couldn't go through with it, knowing what Jenna really thought of him. Let the Maddox Hill Board of Directors fire him, if that was what they needed to do. He'd survive. He wouldn't get to helm the Beyond Earth projects, or any of the other large-scale eco-building projects he'd been working toward, but too damn bad. Life wasn't fair.

With his reputation, he'd always find work. He could go someplace far away. New York, Toronto, London, Singapore, South Africa. Sydney, maybe. He'd start fresh. Try the whole damn thing again. From the top.

When the sky had lightened to a sullen charcoal gray, he gave up even trying to sleep. He took a long shower and made coffee, pondering how to inform his sister that her crazy reality show had run its course. The board could vote as they pleased. Uncle Malcolm could rant and rave. Harold could gloat and rub his hands together. Drew would be on a plane, jetting away from it all.

He could open his own company. Maybe get Vann and Zack to come with him. He'd served with them in Iraq, and then convinced them to come to Maddox Hill with him. Vann was chief financial officer, the youngest the firm had ever had, and Zack was chief security officer. Both were excellent at their jobs.

Come to think of it, maybe he should leave his friends' perfectly successful professional careers alone and not appeal to their loyalty and drag them along with him just because he wanted company in exile. *Grow the hell up, Maddox.*

The world had been trying to tell him that for a while. It was time to listen.

Ava would be furious, but Jenna would probably be relieved, after last night's cringe-worthy leave-taking. This whole thing could so easily become a huge embarrassment for her. She had to regret agreeing to it in the first place.

He showered and shaved, and had just enough time to draft a letter of resignation and put it into his briefcase before he got on the road. Traffic was no worse than usual, and he'd left plenty of time to get there. He got lucky with a parking spot, too, so he was right on schedule when he walked into the Ruby Café.

Ava and her crew were there already, occupying two tables in the back. Ava spotted him and jumped up. She was in work mode, in black jeans and a long, tight-fitting red sweater, black combat boots and red lipstick. Her hair was twisted up into a messy bun. She lifted her tablet and waved it at him triumphantly, and his heart sank.

"Good morning, big brother," she sang out. "You hit the jackpot!"

God, no. His jaw clenched until it cramped. "What's the damage?"

"Who said anything about damage? I'm talking priceless free viral publicity! Get that mopey-ass look off your handsome face and sit down. I'll grab you some coffee while you admire my handiwork."

Drew sank down into the chair and glanced at the headlines on the screen. The pictures jolted him. All different angles of the passionate lip-lock with Jenna after escaping from the lobby of the Maddox Hill building. He was looming over her, clutching her like a conquering hero while she arched back in sweet surrender.

Whoa. Hot.

The headlines made him flinch. "Lust-Crazed Architect Romances Sexy Scientist" was one. Then, "Bad Boy of Architecture Locks Lips with Brainiac Beauty of Biomed." And another gem: "Already? Billionaire Starchitect Frolics with Brand-New Plaything."

Ouch. They'd surpassed themselves this time.

Drew shoved the papers away, dismayed. So Jenna wasn't getting out of this unscathed. At best, she'd look foolish and gullible, and at worst...

Never mind. He'd worry about the worst when it crawled down his throat.

Ava set down a fragrant, steaming mug of coffee in front of him and perched on the table next to him. "So?" she said, eyes expectant.

"So what?" he said sourly. "So Jenna's reputation is rolling downhill right after mine, and picking up speed. You want me to celebrate that?"

Ava rolled her eyes. "You're missing the point. Bev is completely taken with Jenna. Hendrick won't do anything to displease her. The board doesn't meet for another week. If we scramble, that's more than enough time to distract, deflect and dazzle, because Jenna is dazzling, right? Is she not the best?"

"Ava," he began grimly, "I've been thinking about this all night, and I've decided that—"

"Wait! Hold that thought. There she is, the Brainiac Beauty of Biomed herself!" Ava bounced up and was gone.

Drew turned, bracing himself.

Ava had her arms wrapped tightly around Jenna's neck, and was jumping excitedly up and down, which made Jenna's corona of bouncing red-gold ringlets toss and flop. When Jenna finally detached herself, smiling, her hazel eyes flicked over to his.

The buzz of that eye contact brought every detail of yesterday's encounter back to his mind. He could smell her scent, feel her softness. Taste the sweet flavors of her lips, her mouth. The way her hair felt wound around his fingers. The way pleasure made her shudder and gasp and move.

His face got hot. His lower body stirred.

He hung back, not wanting to get in her face if she felt self-conscious about last night, but there was no need. Jenna hung up her coat, ignoring him. She was dressed in a black wool sweater that hugged her curves, and a pencil skirt. A narrow gold belt accented her trim waist. Black tights. Lace-up boots with pointy toes, perfect for kicking a lightweight playboy's ass right into an alternate dimension. Her hair was free, a mane of bouncing curls. No twisting or braiding or bunning today.

"Good morning," he ventured cautiously.

Her eyes flicked to his briefly. "Morning." Her voice was offhand. Remote.

"Sit, sit," Ava urged. "Look at these!" She snatched the tablet away from Drew and presented it to Jenna. "Behold, the magic is happening. Check it out! Superhot, huh? You guys really rocked the method acting. So real! Rawr!"

"Oh, my God." Jenna scrolled through the articles, pausing on each of the pictures. "Wow," she whispered. "That's…really something."

"I know, right?" Ava crowed. "You brainiac beauty, you! Rupert's going to choke on his bran flakes. And only Kayleigh will be there to perform the Heimlich maneuver on him. The poor guy's done for."

Jenna snorted. "I doubt that Rupert follows these particular news channels."

"Oh, you better believe he has his system set to ping if your name is mentioned, that jealous little user. He's always been jealous that you're a better engineer than he is. He couldn't marry you, Jenn, because he wants to *be* you."

Jenna scanned one of the articles, a frown of concentration between her eyes. "Wow. I've never been described as a plaything before. It's like getting written up on a toilet stall in the guys' bathroom. For a good time, call so-and-so. It's a twisted compliment of sorts, but what do you do with it?"

"Enjoy it," Ava suggested. "Accept it. You might as well. What's the alternative?"

"But how do playthings even dress? Higher heels? Shorter skirts? Longer nails, brighter lipstick? Should I giggle and squeal?"

Ava snorted. "Like Kayleigh, you mean?"

"Who's Kayleigh?" Drew asked.

Jenna's mouth tightened. "My ex's twenty-three-year-old intern," she said. "Now his wife. Currently on a romantic honeymoon on a beach in Bali. I wish them well."

"They deserve each other," Ava said. "Rupert is a big butt-itch, and Kayleigh is a classic plaything. Big empty eyes with nothing behind them. Big oversized boobs."

"Hmm," Jenna said. "So I should stuff my bra? And the glasses have got to go."

"No," Drew blurted out.

Ava and Jenna looked around, startled. "Excuse me?" Jenna said.

"Don't stuff your bra," he said. "You're perfect. And I love the glasses."

Damn. Babbling like an idiot. He had no business weighing in on this. He had a goddamn letter of resignation in his briefcase. "Which brings me to what I wanted to tell the two of you," he said swiftly. "I spent some time last night thinking it over. And I've decided that this whole thing was a big mistake."

Jenna's eyes narrowed behind her glasses. "Oh, really? Why is that?"

Her cool, dispassionate tone confused him. "We don't have time for this crap," he told her. "You, especially. You're doing real work, Jenna. Important work. You've got no business playacting for the paparazzi."

Ava crossed her arms over her chest. "Bite your tongue," she said. "It's working, Drew. It's effortless. I'm pulling all the strings and they're doing all the work. Please remember that it's not all about you. This raises the profile of Arm's Reach, too."

"But is this really the way you want Arm's Reach's profile to be raised?" he asked.

Ava shrugged. "Who cares? You know the old saying 'there is no such thing as bad publicity,' right?"

"Big oversimplification, Av. And you know it, or we wouldn't have this scandal problem to begin with," Drew said. He looked at Jenna. "You're no plaything. Don't bother pretending to be one."

Jenna's eyebrows climbed. "So you're chickening out on me?"

Drew was startled. "Chickening out? What the hell? You mean you actually *want* to continue this farce?"

Jenna shrugged. "Right now, I'm just a sexy play-thing to the tabloids. But if you bail on me, I'll be a failed plaything. A loser plaything. One who sucked so badly at playing, she couldn't even keep the bad boy of architecture entertained for one single night. I can see the headlines already. 'Dumped by the Starchitect.' 'Sorry, Geek-Girl, One and Done.' I'll be an object of pity and scorn."

"Jenna—"

"Bev Hill will be too embarrassed by my patheti-cally bad judgment that she won't even want to look me in the eye, so to hell with any partnership possibilities from the Bricker Foundation," Jenna said. "Of course that won't stop my crusade, but it's still embarrassing." She crossed her arms over her chest. Chin up, staring him down.

Turning him on.

"I just thought, after what you said last night, that you'd be glad to be done with this," he said carefully.

"What?" Ava's gaze sharpened, flicking back and forth between them. "What happened last night?"

"None of your business, Av," he said. "Private con-versation."

Ava's eyes widened. "Excuse me? Private conver-sation? About what? Clue me in, guys. Oh, wait. Am I being a bossy, condescending hag again?"

"Yes, you are, since you asked," Jenna said. "Leave him alone, Ava."

His sister started to laugh. "Oh, man. Again. It's just so cute. I'm dying."

"What's so cute?" Jenna sounded annoyed.

"You two," Ava said. "When you close ranks against me. It's just precious."

His sister kept on talking, but her voice faded into background babble. All he saw was the spark in Jenna's eyes. The jut of her chin, her upright posture. Her tilted eyebrow, silently asking him if he could rise to the challenge.

Oh, hell yeah. He'd already risen, in her honor. In every sense. He let his gaze rove appreciatively over her body. The color deepened in her cheeks, and her gaze slid away.

Good. She was aware of him as a man, no matter how low her opinion of him as a person might be. That was something.

"I give in. I can't bear to see you billed as a failed plaything," he said, leaning over and grabbing one of the breakfast sandwiches. "Let's do this thing."

Jenna pawed through the sandwiches and selected one herself, shooting him a quick, sidelong smile as he took his first bite. Mmm, smoked ham, poached eggs, melted Gruyere cheese on an English muffin. Lots of pepper. The cheese was still hot and gooey.

He suddenly felt like he could eat five of them.

Seven

"I don't understand why I have to wear makeup at all." Michael Wu flinched away from Suzan the makeup artist's bronzer brush. "It tickles, and it smells funny."

"The lights will wash you out, Michael," Jenna explained patiently, for the umpteenth time. "You'll look like a ghost."

"So lemme be a ghost, then. I'm fine with that," Michael shot back, rebellious.

Ava swept in to the rescue, perching on the chair next to him and giving him a coaxing smile. "Come on, Michael," she wheedled. "This video's going to be seen by a lot of people. You've got to look good."

Yay, Ava. Jenna left her to it. Thirteen-year-old Michael had a huge crush on her glamorous friend. It came in handy at times like these.

She glanced back when she heard Michael laughing.

He was already getting his cheeks bronzed by Suzan, talking animatedly to Ava. Damn, she loved that kid.

Today, she had her three most experimental cases on display, all of whom had benefited from the expensive preparatory surgeries that had been funded by the AI and Robotics International Award. Michael had lost both arms to meningitis septicemia, one above the elbow and one below, but with the sensory reinnervation surgery, which had rerouted the nerves that had originally run down to his fingers onto the skin above his stumps, Michael now had nervous impulses running both ways. He could command the prostheses at will, and get actual sensory feedback from the sensors. Pressure, texture, grip force, heat and cold. With ferocious practice, he'd achieved remarkable motor control.

Roddy Hepner and Cherise Kurtz were the other two featured in Ava's video. Roddy was a Marine who had lost an arm in an IED blast in Afghanistan. Right now, he was seated on one of the couches by the wall talking with Drew, having already submitted, if reluctantly, to Suzan's bronzing and shading.

Drew was speaking as she approached. "…in Fallujah. First Infantry Battalion. I was the squad leader of an M252 mortar platoon."

Roddy nodded sagely. "You got wounded during Operation Phantom Fury, then?"

"No, that happened later, in Ramadi. I took a couple bullets to the back. One of them fractured my L-5 vertebra and lodged in the spinal canal, so I spent the next few months at Walter Reed. I'm lucky I can walk." Drew paused. "And that I'm alive."

"Me, too. I started out in Landstuhl and then got shipped to San Antonio." Roddy noticed her, and a huge smile split his bushy dark beard. "Hey, Prof! They tell me you're engaged to this dude. Who knew? You're breaking my heart!"

"Sorry about your heart," Jenna told him. "Word travels fast."

"Well, if it can't be me, at least you picked a Marine," Roddy said philosophically. "Way better than that last guy you had. That dude had no discernible balls at all."

She laughed at him. "Did you tell Drew about your music?"

"Yeah, I was telling him how the team here worked out some extra attachments for my arm for the drumsticks, and we're working on more bounce and flex for drumming. I've been practicing like a maniac. My roommates wanna kill me, but I can do crazy polyrhythms now that two-handed drummers can't even dream of doing." His grin flashed again. "First, the Seattle music scene. Then, world domination."

"Roddy writes his own music," Jenna told Drew. "He gave me a demo with some of his original songs, and they're gorgeous."

Roddy's smile faded a notch. "Yeah, well. That demo was recorded back when I could still play bass, guitar and keyboards. I laid down all those tracks myself. But I can still write songs, and sing 'em, even if I can't play the chords. Say, Prof, if you invite me to your wedding, I'll play your favorite song for your first dance. What's the one you liked so much? It was 'Thirsting for You,' right?"

There was a brief, embarrassed silence, during which Jenna couldn't look at Drew.

Roddy chuckled and waved his prosthetic arm at her. "Aw, don't sweat it. Cherise said your guy is, like, a rich famous architect, so it'll probably be a string-quartet-playing-Mozart kind of wedding, right? That's cool. I don't judge you. And I dig Mozart."

By now, Jenna had reordered her wits. "No, Roddy, not at all. There is nothing I would rather have for my first dance than you performing 'Thirsting for You,'" she said, with absolute sincerity. "We're on, buddy. Whenever and wherever it happens."

"Aw, shucks." Roddy grinned, but his gaze flicked speculatively from her to Drew and back again. "Maybe you should play my demo for your guy first," he advised. "He might not groove to my gritty country-rock vibe. It's all good, either way, got it?"

"I like gritty country rock," Drew told them. "I'd love to hear your stuff."

"Awesome, then. Jenna has the audio files," Roddy told him. "She can set you up."

"Great," Drew said. "I'd like to hear you. Do you play anywhere around town?"

Roddy's face fell. "Not yet," he admitted. "Haven't had much luck getting gigs since I came back without my arm. I did better when I could play four different instruments. Now I just got drums and vocals. And with only one arm, well… It's hard. Club owners, well. They don't look past that. I can't catch a break. Not yet."

"Tell me about it, man."

They all turned to see Cherise Kurtz, the third star in Ava's video series. Her makeup was gloriously done, as she was the only one to give Suzan full rein. In the last video, her hair had been teal green. This time, it was shaved tight on the sides with a long forelock dangling over her eye that shaded from pink to a deep purple.

"Love the hair," Roddy said admiringly. "You're the baddest babe, Cher."

"You know it, big guy." They fist-bumped carefully, their prostheses making a clickety sound. Twenty-five-year-old Cherise, an aspiring commercial artist and graphic designer, had lost her right arm to bone cancer. Her goal was to be able to draw again.

Cherise seized Jenna in a tight hug, patting her back with the prosthetic arm. "Hey, Professor! Ava was telling me you're engaged again! Last I heard, you'd just unloaded that useless tool Rupert. Screw that guy. Onward and upward."

"Absolutely. This is, uh, pretty new," Jenna said, flustered. "Cherise, meet Drew."

Cherise gave Drew a long, lingering once-over, and looked back at Jenna, owl-eyed. "You go, girl," she said in hushed tones. "This one is *fine*."

"Don't overdo it, Cherise," Jenna murmured. "It'll go to his head."

"I'll try to contain myself. Ava said to tell you we can get started. I go first today, boys. Before I start sweating under the lights and my mascara starts to run."

They got underway in front of the cameras. Jenna started by filming the process of fitting the sensor map sleeve over Cherise's stump. Then they attached the muscle-reading ring, and fitted the prosthesis directly onto the titanium plug emerging from her stump that she had gotten in the osseointegration surgery. It allowed the prosthesis to attach directly to the bone without stressing her skin. Twist, *click*, and it was in place.

"Flex, and clench," Jenna directed.

Cherise did so smoothly.

"Thumb to every fingertip," Jenna directed.

Cherise did so: *tap, tap, tap, tap.* Then back again, swiftly and smoothly.

"Excellent," Jenna said, delighted. "Your control improves every time."

"You better believe it," Cherise said fervently. "I practice sixteen hours every damn day with this thing. I want my life back."

"What is it that you want to do?" Drew asked.

"I'd just applied to a bunch of graphic design schools last year when I got diagnosed," Cherise told him. "I got distracted. But I'm not giving up. Let me show you this latest thing I've been working on."

They moved closer, along with the cameramen, as Cherise hoisted up a big folder. She laid it on the table, struggling for a few seconds to open it with her prosthetic fingers.

When she finally got it open, she showed them a series of bold-colored drawings of prosthetic arms like her own, with various decorations superimposed on them.

"I have a bunch of ideas," she said, leafing through them. "These are just a few. This is Fairy Kingdom. This is Thunder Dragon. Then there's Skull Snake, Sith Lord, Starsong, Elven Realm, and this is my favorite, Goblin King. You put these on with a light adhesive so they can be switched out easily whenever you need a different look."

"Those are amazing, Cherise," Jenna said. "What a great idea."

"You drew these with your prosthetic hand?" Drew asked.

"Yes. I'm slow, but it's getting better, bit by bit. I'm training my left hand, too." Cherise looked at Jenna. "I want to propose a series of decorations for the prosthesis for your brochure and your online catalog. Amputees need to make fashion statements, too."

"Great idea," Jenna said. "We'll discuss it."

"I also really need for you guys to put some sort of base to apply decorative fingernails to the prosthesis," Cherise said. "A girl needs her fingernails."

"We're on it," Jenna promised.

"Was this project in your design school application portfolio?" Drew asked.

"No, I applied before I started these," she replied. "I've already got a bunch of rejection letters in my collection. You gotta hang on to those, you know? Every good success story has a big fat wad of rejection letters in it."

"A project like this would attract their attention," Drew said. "I bet they don't see this level of dedication and commitment every day."

"Aw." Cherise beamed at him. "Thanks, handsome. You made my day." She looked over at Jenna and mimed fanning herself vigorously. *Lucky girl,* she mouthed.

Jenna felt a clutch in her throat. It felt just as wrong to fake an engagement with Drew in front of Cherise and Roddy as it had in front of Bev. It felt disrespectful to misrepresent something that important to people whom she loved and respected.

But she'd recommitted to this strange charade herself, in the café this morning. And she'd deliberately goaded Drew into recommitting to it, too. All because being the failed plaything had stung her pride. Wow. Talk about shallow.

Nothing to do now but grit her teeth and tough it out.

Eight

Drew watched Roddy's segment with intense interest, amazed at the dexterity the other man had developed with the drumsticks.

He was impressed. Not just by the accomplishments of Jenna and her team, but also by his sister. He'd known in a general way what she did for a living, but he'd never seen her actively doing it. Ava had the air of a seasoned professional who knew what she wanted and how to get it, and she was effortlessly authoritative. Her crew snapped to it because they wanted to please her.

He could never let her know this, however. His bratty and annoying little sister was already insufferable and nearly impossible to manage. No need to fan the flames.

He got out of their way while they were setting up for the next segment. At the far end of the crowded, busy room, a skinny adolescent boy with two prosthetic arms sat on one of the couches. His black hair was buzzed off, and he was wearing an oversize *Angel Ascending* T-shirt. Two women flanked him on either side who had to be his mother and grandmother. The women looked like older and younger versions of each other, both short and slight and with long hair pulled back, the mom's into a braid, the grandma's into a bun. The mom's hair was black, the grandma's snow white.

Drew nodded politely at them as he addressed the kid. "You're Michael, right?" He gestured at the T-shirt. "You like *Angel Ascending*?"

The boy's eyes lit up. "Yeah. Cool game."

"Did you see the movie?"

"It was awesome," he said. "Lars Feehan is the bomb."

They were discussing the game they both played, though Michael had made it several levels beyond Drew, despite his prosthetic arms. Jenna appeared beside them and waited, smiling at Michael's enthusiasm.

"You gotta watch the YouTube gamer videos for clues if you want to make progress," Michael instructed him. "That was how I learned about the ancient scroll and the dimensional portal. Oh, hey, Jenna."

"Hey, Michael." She gave Michael's mother and grandmother a smile. "Hi, Joyce. Hello, Mrs. Wu. Michael, how are the flexibility adjustments working out for you? Is the writing and typing going better?"

"Not enough of the writing and typing is going at all, in my opinion." Joyce cast a stern eye at her son. "All he practices is gaming."

Michael rolled his eyes. "Not true, Mom. It's going fine. So far so good."

"Let's go take a look," Jenna said, beckoning.

Drew followed them all back to the spotlighted zone where the cameramen were waiting, hanging back to stay out of the way, but watching in fascination as Jenna and her team did the sequence of preparations on Michael's stumps; adjusting the sensor map sleeve and then snapping on the arms, which were black and chrome-colored.

"Those arms are badass," Drew commented.

Michael shot him a grin. "Yeah. I'm, like, the Terminator."

"Okay, Michael," Jenna said. "Flex…clench…thumb to each fingertip…very good. I can see you've been working hard. Let's test the sensory pads. Close your eyes."

Michael squeezed his eyes shut. "Ready."

Jenna touched his prosthetic hands lightly in a random pattern with her fingertip, and Michael announced each touch. "Right forefinger. Left pinky. Left wrist. Right heel of the hand. Right middle finger. Left ring finger. Right ring finger. Right wrist. Left heel."

"Excellent," Jenna said. "So much better than the last time, which was already impressive."

"Come try the gaming console," Jenna said. "We got it all set up for you."

Michael settled himself in the chair in front of the monitor, the cameramen shifting unobtrusively into place around him, and woke the screen with a stroke on a touchpad with his prosthetic finger and logged into his account. He grinned over his shoulder at his mother. "I can feel the pad now, Mom! I can tell that it's kinda sticky and soft."

"That's great, baby," Joyce told him.

"I'm going to try to make it through a new portal

this time," Michael said to Drew as he picked up the console. "I saved this moment for your video. 'Cause it's, like, dramatic."

"Very generous of you," Ava said.

Michael shot her a mischievous grin over his shoulder as he positioned his mechanical fingers carefully over the buttons. "I know," he said. "Here goes. Wish me luck."

They waited through the logo and opening scenes of *Angel Ascending*. Then Michael's avatar appeared and began to run, bounding like a gazelle across the landscape pictured on the screen, right toward a cliff.

"Okay, here we go," Michael said under his breath. "Full power…and *jump*."

The avatar leaped. Enormous wings unfolded, glinting silver and billowing like a sail, filling with wind currents. The game had begun.

After several minutes of intense play, Michael deftly steered his avatar through the magical membrane of the portals into a blaze of golden light, whooping with joy. "*Yes!* I made it! I'm in level thirteen, and I got dragon wings now! I am killing it! Did you see me, Mom?"

Joyce Wu burst into tears and covered her face with her hands.

Michael turned around, alarmed. "Mom? What's wrong?"

"Sorry, honey," Joyce said, her voice strangled. "I'm just… I haven't seen you look that happy in a long time."

"Aw, Mom. Don't." Michael launched himself at his mother. He wrapped his prosthetic arms around her, patting her carefully. One of the hands landed on her long braid. He closed his mechanical fingers around it and tugged on it gently.

"I can feel your hair, Mom," he said, in a wondering voice.

That just made her cry harder. Drew had a lump in his own throat. Then he felt something soft bump into him from the side. Thin, wiry arms wound around him.

It was the elderly Mrs. Wu, also weeping. She, too, needed to hug someone, and he was the closest person. Whatever. He wrapped his arms around the old lady, because what else could he do? Over her white hair, he caught Ava's smile as she gestured silently for one of her cameramen to capture the moment.

Then he saw Jenna's face, and promptly forgot everything and everyone else.

She was beaming at him. Her eyes were wet. She took off her glasses, dabbed below her eyes and then sniffed into a tissue.

What a beautiful, radiant smile. It gave him an amazing rush. He could get used to this.

He wanted to chase down smiles like that every day. Endlessly. He could dedicate himself to that project and never get tired of it.

Mrs. Wu didn't let go, but nothing could embarrass him when he was flying so high from Jenna's smile. He embraced the elder Mrs. Wu as carefully as if he were holding a baby bird, and just breathed it all in. Letting himself feel it.

He hadn't felt this good in…well, damn. Maybe never.

Mrs. Wu finally let go of him with a motherly pat on his back. He caught Michael's eyes, which were also suspiciously wet. "You play *Angel Ascending* in online mode, right?" Drew asked, on impulse.

"Yeah, sure," Michael said. "As much as Mom will let me."

"I know I'd have to up my game to play with you, but let's hook up online. I usually play after midnight when I can't sleep, but I could move it up a couple hours."

"More like four hours," Joyce announced. "He has to be in bed by ten thirty."

"Mom!" Michael shot her a mortified look. "As if!"

"Done by ten thirty, always," Drew agreed. "Hey, I play with Lars Feehan sometimes. He's a night owl, too, like me."

Michael's eyes went huge. "No way! Lars Feehan the actor? Who starred in the *Angel Ascending* movie? He games? For real?"

"For real," Drew said. "Whenever he can. He's good, too. Last I checked, he'd just cracked level eight, but that was a while ago. He might have moved up since then."

Jenna's eyes were wide with startled wonder. "You know Lars Feehan?"

"Yeah. I designed his producer's beach house a few years ago. Maybe we could all three hook up online and play sometime."

"Lars…freaking… Feehan!" Michael repeated, his eyes still dazzled. "The gold angel! That guy is so cool!"

"Yeah, and if you hook him up with Lars, we get to film it, okay?" Ava said pointedly. "The guy has thirty million Twitter followers."

"I'm sure he'll be up for that," Drew said. "He's a great guy."

"You play video games with Lars Feehan?" Jenna said. "The Hollywood A-list hottie and the bad boy of architecture, two of the busiest guys in their respective professions, have time to play video games together in the middle of the night?"

He sure did. It helped during those long and sleepless nights when nightmares and stress flashbacks kicked his ass. But that was nobody's business.

"Video games relax me," he said, defensively. "They're a great de-stressor."

"Dude. Don't even try to make her understand." Michael's voice sounded world-weary. "If she doesn't game herself, she just won't get it. They all just say, 'Oh, you're rotting your brain,' or 'Oh, you're wasting precious time that you'll never, ever get back,' blah-blah-blah."

"True," one of the cameramen agreed wryly. "That's what my wife says."

"Well, people. Be that as it may." Ava clapped her hands. "I think we have what we need for the day. Thanks, everyone. You were beyond fabulous. Until next time."

Then came a big round of emotional hugs, from which Drew was by no means exempt. "I'll look for you online," he told Michael.

"Look for CyborgStrong8878." The teenager gave him a tight, shaking hug and then hurried out with his mom and grandma on either side, chattering excitedly.

Drew figured that he was technically free to go himself, after the Wu family, Cherise and Roddy had all left, but still he lingered watching Ava's crew pack up. He wasn't ready for the whole experience to be over, and Jenna had disappeared from the room a few minutes ago. He didn't want to leave until he said goodbye to her, and maybe got another one of those gorgeous smiles as a farewell gift.

Then Jenna and Ava reappeared. Ava was on her cell phone, and she spotted him and waved him over, still talking as he approached.

"You diabolical schemer, you. A man after my own heart. I'll let them know." She pocketed her phone. "Okay, my lovelies. Time to get back to my workshop and start postproduction. That was Ernest, and he wants you to know that A, he called in some favors to get you two a reservation at Piepoli's for eight, and B, news of this dinner reservation has been discreetly leaked to our favorite paparazzi. A few of them should bite."

"Paparazzi? I don't feel camera ready right now." Jenna looked doubtful.

"Nonsense," Ava said briskly. "You've been thoroughly worked over by Suzan, the makeup goddess, and you look beautiful. Let's keep up the pressure, people."

"Too much pressure," Drew said. "It's been a long day, Av. Let her rest."

"You still have to eat, right?" his sister pointed out. "So multitask."

Drew looked at Jenna. "No pressure," he told her. "At least not from me. I could take you straight home, or to some other restaurant where you could relax in peace and privacy. Your call. No one else's."

Ava sighed sharply. "Don't be difficult, Drew. I'm going to a lot of trouble here."

He kept his eyes on Jenna. "Don't push her around."

His sister snorted. "You know you're just egging me on when you defend her, right?"

"I'm ignoring you," he said calmly. "And Jenna decides on her own dinner plans."

Jenna gave him one of those smiles that blew his

mind. "I've heard great things about the lobster ravioli at Piepoli's," she said. "I'm up for some of that."

"Yes!" Ava clapped her friend on the back. "That's the spirit! All you need to do is pretend to enjoy each other's company while eating a fabulous meal. No sweat."

Jenna shrugged, her gaze darting away from his. "I'm, ah, sure we'll manage."

Drew looked at the color blooming on Jenna's cheeks, longing to touch it. Feel the soft heat. She'd made her boundaries plain, but he still wanted more of her attention.

As much of it as he could get.

Nine

Jenna felt like she was floating as she followed the waiter through the bustling restaurant. She'd lived in this town five years and she'd never yet managed to get a table at Piepoli's. But around Drew, all kinds of impossible things became possible.

Effortless, even. He knew Lars Feehan? Seriously?

The day's emotional intensity had left Jenna feeling dangerously unshielded, but for some reason, she'd still jumped on the chance to have dinner with Drew. She didn't care if his sister had maneuvered him into it, or if he was doing it for his own selfish ends. Who cared? Tonight, she just wanted to sit across a candlelit table from Drew Maddox and drink him in. This was her chance to look her fill. Listen to his beautiful, resonant voice.

He'd been so sweet with Michael. She was beyond charmed. She'd melted into sniffling, laughing-through-her-tears goo.

And it was a bad time to lower her guard. She was putting herself in temptation's way. Throwing fuel on the fire. She was a smart woman, and she knew better, but tonight, she just…didn't…care.

The waiter seated them at a table by the window that overlooked the boardwalk outside.

"Don't look now," Drew said. "Our friends are already outside, snapping pictures."

"I guess you must be used to this by now, right?"

"More like indifferent. I barely notice them, unless they're bothering you. Here." He seized her hand. "I'll give them a dose of what they like best."

She gasped and laughed at him as he kissed her knuckles, then turned it over and kissed her palm. Intense awareness of him raced through every part of her body.

"I'm impressed that you can be so relaxed about it." She struggled to keep her voice even.

"There are worse things," he said.

Drew's tone was light, but she knew enough from Ava about what he'd been through in the military to guess what he was thinking. "You mean Iraq?"

He nodded. "I saw things there I won't ever forget. A few times, I thought it was the end of me. Once you've taken enemy fire or had your convoy blown up, people snapping pictures of you no longer registers on your radar as an actual problem."

"Ava told me you'd been wounded," she said. "I overheard you talking to Roddy about it today."

"Yeah. A bullet fractured one of my lumbar vertebrae and lodged next to my spine. That was the end of my time in the Marine Corps. I'm lucky that I can walk, and that I'm alive. I think about that every day."

"I can imagine," Jenna said. "A bullet to the spine? It must have been so painful."

"It was. Three surgeries. Months of recovery. It puts everything else into perspective."

"I bet it does," she murmured.

"I got into video games during my recovery, after I got home," he told her. "My convalescence was long and boring, and it hurt. Video games take your mind off things."

"Did you play that game that Michael showed us during your recovery?"

"Oh, no. *Angel Ascending* is much more recent. Lars sent me that last year after the movie opened, just for laughs. He's a really good guy. I'll introduce you sometime."

She laughed. "Wow, lucky me. Lifestyles of the rich and famous."

"I suppose. We're all the same when it comes to the important stuff. Getting shot in the back teaches you that. No matter how privileged you might be, you're never exempt from pain, or death. Keeps you honest." He paused. "Sorry," he said, self-consciously. "Didn't mean to get all heavy and self-involved on you."

"I don't see it that way at all," she said. "I've worked with veterans."

"I bet you have," he said.

She squeezed his hand, which she was still holding. "You were wonderful with Michael today. Roddy and Cherise, too. Michael was so excited."

"He's a great kid," Drew said. "Entirely apart from how he's overcoming the challenges he faces."

"That he is," she agreed. "I just love him. So funny. He has a great attitude."

"They all impressed me," Drew said reflectively. "The whole damn thing impressed me. Your techniques, your team, your tech, your lab. Even my sister impressed me today. Just don't ever tell her I said so."

Jenna laughed. "I won't. And thanks, that's good to hear. Now I just need to make the techniques affordable for everyone who needs them."

The waiter arrived, and they gave him their order. After the wine had been served, Jenna asked Drew a question she'd wondered about ever since she first met him. "I'm curious about something," she said. "How did you end up joining the Marines? It's not an obvious choice. Being a Maddox and all."

Drew's eyes narrowed thoughtfully as he considered his reply. "Long story."

"We're not in a hurry," she remarked.

He sipped his wine. "I don't know how much Ava told you," he said. "But after my parents were killed in that plane accident, I went sort of wild."

Sort of? Ha. That was a massive understatement.

"Ava did mention that," she murmured.

"That was my way of coping. I was pissed at my folks for dying. I didn't care about consequences. So I got into a lot of trouble. It was lucky I was a juvenile offender, and that I never actually hurt anyone. But Uncle Malcolm was beside himself. You saw how he is. He got in my face, made threats and ultimatums. He got my back up, to the point that I wasn't in the mood to trot off to college like a good boy, study hard and make him proud. I wanted to raise hell. So I joined the Marines. First Division, First Battalion. Ended up in Iraq. I learned some very important things there."

"Such as?"

He was silent for a long moment. "No need to raise hell," he said simply. "I was already there."

Jenna nodded and stayed quiet, waiting for him to go on.

"I saw a lot of bad things," he said slowly. "Things I can't forget. But it's not like it was all a nightmare. I worked hard, grew up, learned a lot. Made good friends in my platoon. Two of them work with me right here at Maddox Hill. Vann's my CFO. He's freakishly good with numbers, and Zack is our CSO. Those guys are solid as a rock. I've trusted them both with my life and they have never let me down. In the end, I'd say it was worth it just to have found them."

"You're fortunate to have friends like that," she said. "So after you got wounded, you decided to follow the family architecture tradition?"

"I always knew I'd get there eventually," he admitted. "It was destiny. I grew up around architects. My dad was one, and when I was a kid, he always talked like it was a given that I would be, too. Then after I got shot, I had all these long empty hours to think about my future. By the time I recovered and got to architecture school, I was maniacally focused. I made up for all the lost time."

"I bet Uncle Malcolm was relieved," she said.

"He couldn't believe his luck," Drew said. "Back then, anyway. Now he's changed his tune. Decided that I'm more trouble than I'm worth."

Jenna shook her head. "No. This is all just a blip on your screen. It won't hurt you in the long run."

"I hope you're right," he said. "I had some projects in the works that I was really attached to."

"Anything I might have heard of?"

"We haven't landed them yet, but Maddox Hill is in the running for the Beyond Earth project. I thought a lot about Mars when I was in the Al Anbar Province. Lots of time to stare at the rocks and sand and think about the unique problems inherent in building in environments inhospitable to man. It would involve robotics and three-D printing with local building materials. It's a long shot, with lots of competition, but I have my fingers crossed."

"Wow." She was silent for a moment, digesting it. "That's huge."

"Yeah, it is for me. My dad used to read science fiction stories to me to put me to sleep when I was small. We always said we'd build houses on Mars together someday."

That made her throat tighten up. She couldn't reply.

"I'd hate to miss out on that chance," he said. "He would have gotten such a kick out of that. If I ever do manage to pull it off, it'll be in his honor."

Fortunately for her, the lobster ravioli arrived, and food took center stage for a while. The ravioli were tender and plump and fabulous, the wine was excellent, and Drew was great company. By the time dessert and coffee arrived, the elements of the evening had combined into a magical alchemy that made her relaxed and giggly and mellow.

Then Drew glanced outside at the walkway. "Persistent bastards," he murmured. "I was kind of hoping they'd get bored and go home, but there they still are. Hanging in there."

Jenna looked out the window, realizing that she'd completely forgotten about the photographers. Which was to say, she'd forgotten the whole reason they'd come to this restaurant in the first place.

She laughed to cover her embarrassment. "Want me to do something crazy and dramatic to entertain them? I could throw a glass of wine in your face."

He grinned. "It's a little early in our relationship for that."

"I could feed you a bite of my *sporcamuss*," she said, spooning up a bite of the delicious, goopy puff pastry with cream. "That fits the narrative, as Ava would say."

He accepted the bite, and savored it. "Mmm. Wow. Good."

Whew. That smile of sensual promise unraveled something inside her. She felt like she was teetering on the brink of something dangerous and wonderful in equal measures.

Oh, boy. This was bad. She'd been prepared to be dazzled by his looks, impressed by his smarts, wowed by his talent, allured by his seductive charm. Those reactions were all foreseen and adjusted for. She was being smart. Taking care of herself, like a grown-up.

But she hadn't expected to like him this much.

That was a dirty trick.

Ten

No one ever, in the history of dining, had made a cup of espresso last as long as Drew did after they finished their dessert. He didn't want that perfect day to end.

He'd been with a lot of women, in his time, and he'd made it his business to be good at pleasing them, appreciating them, seeing them, knowing them. But apart from the sex, he'd never felt like anyone had ever successfully known him back.

Some women had tried, to their credit. He'd always assumed it was his fault when they failed. A mysterious personality defect on his part. His defenses were too high, he couldn't let anyone inside, yada-yada-yada. Big shame, but what could you do.

But he'd been open to Jenna from the start. Wide open. No choice about it. The intimacy of it stirred him up, made him feel shaky and off balance.

It was strange, how much he liked it.

Drew dealt with the bill, and they went outside and strolled together down to the street. The wind coming off the sound was raw and cold, whipping a hot pink color into her cheeks and tossing her curls wildly.

Then they were holding hands. He didn't remember deciding to do it. It felt as if the natural state of their hands was to be clasped.

She glanced up at him. "Are the photographers still following us?"

"No idea," he said. "Didn't think to look."

"Ah. So you're staying in character just in case?"

That stung, a little. "I suppose," he said. "Didn't really think of it that way."

"Hey, wait," Jenna said. "Drew, wasn't that your car? Back there behind us?"

Drew turned to look. She was right. He'd walked right past it. Lost in space.

He unlocked his black Jag with the key fob and opened the door for her.

Jenna backed away, flustered and smiling and holding her hands up. "Oh, no. That's not necessary. I'll call a car. It'll save you an hour of pointless driving."

"I can't just leave you here," he told her. "Please. Get in. Let me take you home."

She sighed, but got in without further argument, to his immense relief.

Once they were on their way, having his eyes on the road ahead instead of on her made the question he'd been wanting to ask her come out more easily.

"This mission to help amputees get the use of their hands back, it seems like more than a career for you," he commented. "It seems very personal. What's that all about?"

Jenna was quiet for a long moment, so he started looking at her profile, trying to gauge if he'd over-stepped some boundary.

"It is personal," she said. "My brother Chris lost an arm to bone cancer, just like Cherise. They amputated his right arm right above the elbow."

"That must have been hard," he said.

"He was only eighteen. I was twelve. He'd just won a big basketball scholarship, right before he was diag-nosed. He was a very gifted athlete."

He winced. "Oh, God. That hurts."

"Yeah, it broke everyone's hearts that he had to give up that dream."

"What does he think of your line of work? Does he have one of your magic arms?"

Jenna was silent again. This time for so long that he suddenly guessed, in a flash of total dismay, what she was going to say and cursed himself for being so damn clumsy.

"We lost Chris about a year after that operation," Jenna said. "They didn't catch it in time. They found it in his spine, his liver. He did chemo and all that, but it got him."

He just let that sit for a moment before he said, "I'm so sorry." He wished there was something less trite and shopworn to say, but there never freaking was.

"Thanks," she murmured.

They were silent for a long time, but he finally gath-ered his courage and gave it another shot. "How about your parents? What's their story?"

She shook her head. "My dad was never in the picture. He left not long after I was born. My mom raised us on her own. But she never quite came back to herself, after losing Chris. She struggled for years. Then she had a heart attack six years ago. So it's just me now." She gave him a brief smile. "Something we have in common. Both orphaned."

He nodded. "That's why you do this work, right? You want to give to all these people what you couldn't give to Chris?"

Jenna gazed down at her hands clasped on her lap. "I suppose," she said. "Hadn't ever thought of it like that. Chris was my North Star, I guess. The whole world needs to be saved, and no one can save it all, since we're not comic book superheroes. But if we all do a little, maybe we have a chance. And this is my bit. Someone else can work on saving the whales and the bees and the ozone and the ocean. I'm doing the arms."

"You make me want to save the world, too," he said. "I feel like such a slacker."

She laughed at him. "Ha! You just keep doing what you're doing. Your buildings are gorgeous. You're helping make sustainable eco-friendly urban planning a reality in cities all over the world. Beautiful things make the whole world better."

He felt both embarrassed and ridiculously pleased. "Thanks."

He parked in front of her apartment and turned off the engine.

Tension gripped them. They were in the danger zone again. Every detail of last night's passionate episode, and its painful aftermath, hung heavy in the air between them.

"I really want to walk upstairs with you and see you

safely inside," he said. "But I will not come on to you. I swear it. On my honor."

"That's really not necessary," she murmured.

"What? Walking you upstairs, or swearing sacred vows on my honor?"

"Both. You're being overdramatic. But if it makes you feel better, fine."

He walked her up and stopped when he saw her front door, mindful of his vow.

Jenna drifted reluctantly onward toward her door. "Good night," she said. "Thanks for everything. The ride, dinner. And for making Michael's day. It was so sweet of you."

"Don't thank me," he said. "This was a great day for me. Best day I've had in longer than I can even remember."

I could make it the best night, too.

The unsaid words vibrated between them, because apparently he hadn't learned last night's lesson well enough. The longing to touch her just kept getting stronger.

"It was wonderful for me, too," she admitted.

They gazed at each other. This was his cue, to say something lighthearted. Repeat the good-nights. Turn the hell around. Walk down the damn stairs. Left foot, right foot.

But his voice was locked in his throat. And he made no move to go.

Jenna looked tormented. "Please," she whispered. "Please, Drew. Stop that."

He knew exactly what she meant, but all he could do was play dumb. "I'm not doing or saying anything."

To his dismay, her face crumpled, and she covered it with both her hands, cursing.

He reached out. "Oh, damn. Jenna—"

"No!" She jerked back, out of range, and wiped at her eyes. "No, I'd really better not. Sorry. It's been an emotional day. I'm wrecked."

"I wish I could help," he said.

Jenna looked miserable. "I'm so sorry about what I said last night. The problem is, my reasons for saying it haven't changed." Her voice shook. "I'm extremely attracted to you, as I'm sure you've noticed, and this is hard, and awful. I'm so sorry. But I just…can't."

Ouch. He turned away before she could see the look on his face. "Okay," he said. "I'm gone. I won't put you on the spot like this."

He ran down the stairs. He felt like he'd been punched in the chest as he started up the car.

For God's sake, look at him. So last night's slap-down hadn't been enough punishment for him. He just had to come back for more. He'd practically begged her for it.

Women came on to him all the time. There was an art to steering around them, evading them, letting them down gently. He'd considered himself good at it.

The irony was painful. He'd finally found a woman he wanted to get closer to, and she'd slammed the door on him. She thought he was a train wreck waiting to happen.

It would be almost funny, if it didn't suck so hard.

Eleven

"Stop bugging me, Av," Jenna said testily. "My black-and-white gown will be fine for the presentation dinner. It looks good on me. It was expensive. We do not need to shop for another damn dress. End of story."

Ava picked a hunk of artichoke out of her salad and popped it into her mouth. "Sorry to contradict you, but you are so very wrong."

"Why? Why shell out all this money? My closet is full of nice clothes."

"You're being difficult just to be difficult. That dress is old, and done." Ava rolled her eyes at Drew. "Drew, tell your lovely fiancée that she needs a gorgeous new evening gown for the exhibit dinner at the Whitebriar Club, okay?"

"Of course she needs a new evening gown." Drew's voice was offhand. "And this is a Maddox Hill event, so it's only fair you let me pick up the tab for it. I'll give you my credit card. Knock yourselves out. Send me hot photos from the fitting room."

Jenna tried not to flinch. She stared down at her seafood salad, which she'd barely touched. Drew had been like that with her all morning. Pleasant. Polite. And completely emotionally absent.

They'd done yet another interview this morning with a podcast whose online audience was growing fast. The latest of many PR events. Too many. Ava's punishing schedule was exhausting her. The idea today had been to grab an early lunch before everyone went back to work, but Drew's friendly, indifferent blandness had killed her appetite.

She just…freaking…hated it. With all of her heart and soul. And she had no one to blame for it but herself.

"I'm putting my foot down," she said through her teeth. "No new dress."

Ava made a frustrated sound.

"Save it, Av." Drew signaled the waiter for the check. "It's not a good time to discuss it. Obviously."

"Oh, whatever." Ava shrugged, her face rebellious. "But hey. Big news." Ava's voice was elaborately casual. "We heard from the producers of *Angel Ascending*."

Jenna put down her fork, her nerves buzzing with alarm. "You did?"

"Yes. They want to feature Michael in the ad campaign for next year's game."

Jenna sucked in a sharp breath and gazed at Ava's triumphant face, heart thudding hard. "Careful, Av," she said. "I don't want him exploited. He's just a kid."

Ava sighed. "And here I thought you'd be excited at

how my hard work is doing marvels for raising your organization's profile to stratospheric heights. Silly me."

"I think you're amazing at what you do, don't ever doubt it," Jenna said. "But you're doing your work too well. And I'm scared for Michael."

"Don't worry," Ava soothed. "Joyce and I will both defend him like a couple of pit bulls. It would be a nice chunk of change for his college fund, right? Stanford, MIT, am I right? This is all good, Jenn. Be excited for him. And for Arm's Reach. This is great for his future, and it's great for you, too. Michael will be fine. He's strong, and smart."

"But I wanted him to get back his normal life," she said. "Everyday stuff. Not some high-stress, high-visibility situation where people are constantly trying to use him."

"Oh. You mean, like you?" Ava's voice was crisp. "Are you tired of the limelight, Jenn? Do you think we're using you?"

Jenna locked eyes with her friend…and swallowed the sharp reply that Ava did not deserve. She shook her head. "I'm just tired," she said.

"I know, and I'm sorry about that, but buck up. Be strong. Oh, by the way. Speaking of good things. Roddy told me that he has a gig tonight. He's filling in for the Vicious Rumors' drummer down at the Wild Side. All weekend, starting tonight."

"Yes, he texted me about that," Jenna said. "I'm going to try to catch the first set tonight."

"Alone?" Drew's eyes snapped to her. "At the Wild Side? In that part of town?"

"It's fine," she said. "I'm going to the early set. It's a hip, busy neighborhood."

"You can't go down there all alone." He sounded horrified.

"Certainly I can," she told him. "I don't mind going alone, and I'm sure—"

"No way. I'll take you. Want me to get you at the lab, or pick you up at home?"

Jenna just looked at him, bewildered. "Drew. Don't feel like you have to do this. I'm sure you have better things to do with your evening."

"Not really," he said. "I want to see Roddy play."

It was the first time that Drew had looked her straight in the eyes since that disastrous evening last week, and the blazing directness of his gaze was almost jarring.

She let out a careful breath. "Fine," she said. "I'll meet you at the club. I'll be there around nine thirty."

The waiter brought his card back. Drew got up, gave each of them a businesslike peck on the cheek and left, already focused on whatever came next in his busy day.

Jenna watched him walk away, feeling flat and dull. It had been over a week since that disaster after their dinner date. A stressful, chaotic week jam-packed with activities calculated to jack up Arm's Reach's media profile. She was exhausted, and her work was suffering… But that wasn't the real problem, and she couldn't convince herself that it was.

She'd come to dread seeing Drew. But the problem wasn't because of anything he said. It was what he didn't say. He was unfailingly polite and pleasant. Attentive, thoughtful, gallant. No one could fault him.

He was wearing a perfect-fiancé mask. But now that she'd seen the man beneath, the mask almost offended her. Being kept at arm's length felt like a punishment. Not that she blamed him. Not in the least. She'd demanded herself that he pull back. And that didn't help worth a damn.

On the contrary, it made things worse.

It had been a long time since Drew had seen the inside of a club, but he paid no attention to the strobing lights, the pounding music or the crush of people. People tried to catch his eye, male and female, and he ignored them, having become a ruthless and single-minded scanning-for-Jenna machine. He roved through the place, sensors tuned to her and only her. Scanning for that mane of bright hair, either floating high in an explosive updo or bouncing in a cloud around her head. Cat-eye glasses. The glint of clear bright hazel eyes. Those high cheekbones. That elegant posture. That perfume.

No way could he hear her sweet-toned, sexy voice in this noise, but his ears still strained for the sound of it.

A different band was playing at the moment, not the Vicious Rumors. Roddy wasn't onstage yet. The warm-up band was winding up their last big head-banging number. Still no sign of Jenna. He glanced at his phone again. Still no messages from her.

He started another circuit, cruising the place again from the top, room by room.

Yes. A blaze of yellow light had caught her hair, lighting it up like a flame. He fought his way closer. She was wearing a tight, tailored blue coat, a black wool mini-skirt and those ass-kicking boots.

Next to her was a blazing crest of pink and purple. Cherise, talking excitedly. As he approached, Cherise threw her arms around Jenna's neck and hugged her, pounding her with the prosthetic arm. Which was now decorated by long threads of little lights inside flexible plastic tubes wound artistically around it.

Cherise saw him over Jenna's shoulder and waved excitedly, yelling into Jenna's ear. Jenna turned around and caught sight of him.

Bracing himself never worked. He couldn't get used to the rush it gave him to lock eyes with her. The contact seemed to touch him everywhere. Suddenly, he was turned on.

Exactly what she did not want or welcome from him.

"Hey." He greeted them both with a polite nod. From a safe, secure distance.

Cherise was having none of that. She lunged for him and wrapped him in a big hug.

"Drew!" she crowed into his ear. "You are the bomb!"

"I am?" he said, bemused.

"You totally are! You inspired me! I was telling Jenna about my application to the DeLeon Design Institute! They're, like, the hottest program for commercial art, and when I applied last year, they turned me down flat. But I got to thinking about what you said last week, so I applied again, and this time I included my arm decorations in my portfolio. And they called me in for an interview! The director told me that you forwarded the video link from last week's shoot to her!"

Jenna's searching eyes met his. "I had no idea you had these connections," she yelled over the noise.

"Trix DeLeon and I went to high school together," Drew said. "I just sent Trix a link. That's all."

"Aw, don't deny it, buddy. You helped, whether I get in or not. So thanks."

Cherise hugged him again and planted a loud and smacking kiss on his cheek.

"Hey! Drew!" This time it was Roddy who accosted him. He was looking bright-eyed and excited. "I didn't know you and Jenna were coming! Good to see you, man!"

"Yeah, it was a last-minute thing," he said.

"Hey, now's a great time to play that song for you, whaddaya say?"

"What song do you mean?" Drew asked.

"The one for your first dance, at your wedding!" Roddy yelled. "'Thirsting for You,' remember? I got the Rumors to try it out in our rehearsal this afternoon, just in case, and they liked it. I'll make sure it's in the first set!"

"Hey, look at you, Roddy," Cherise called out. "You're using one of my sleeve decorations. Looks supertough. Good choice."

"Yep, I went with Sith Lord tonight. Decided not to use the light strands, though. Didn't want to draw too much attention to the arm. Could look gimmicky."

"Me, I went with Fairy Kingdom today," Cherise said, holding up her own arm.

"Hey, I gotta go. We're about to go on," Roddy said. "Cherise, come on backstage with me and I'll introduce you to Bose, the bass player." He gave them a conspiratorial grin. "She has a crush on him," he added, in a stage whisper that was more like a shout.

"Nah, I'm just a big fan," Cherise protested. "Later, guys!"

Roddy and Cherise plunged into the crowd and were swiftly lost to sight.

Drew and Jenna looked at each other. She leaned forward and yelled into his ear. "Let's go to the room near the front entrance and get a drink. It's quieter out there."

"Sure." Drew slid his arm into hers, and his body got a tingling jolt of Jenna hyperawareness, even through all the layers of fabric.

They found seats at the bar and placed their orders. One of the problems about having to keep his distance emotionally was that he no longer knew how the hell to start a conversation with her.

"I'm sorry that Ava's schedule is stressing you out," he told her. "She just doesn't know when to stop. It's the source of her superpower. It's also a huge pain in the ass."

"I can't deny that it's working," Jenna said. "My team are over the moon at how much attention Arm's Reach is getting. And this thing with Michael and the *Angel Ascending* producers, well. It's incredible, but I'm just not sure how I feel about it."

"I'm glad something useful is coming of it for you," he said. "I was afraid that all my bad press could be damaging to you."

"Not at all. I think it's more like the spice that makes it interesting. You know. The rum in the eggnog. The hot pepper in the salsa."

He snorted. "I'm glad it's good for something."

The bartender delivered their drinks. Jenna sipped her margarita, and turned to him, frowning thoughtfully. "Can I ask you something?"

"Sure."

"The guy who threw that infamous party, the one where you got photographed," she said. "He's made quite a name for himself."

"Arnold Sobel," he said. "Yes, he has. What about him?"

"I was just wondering why you would hang out with

a guy like that. He doesn't seem your type. Why go to that party in the first place?"

Just mentioning Sobel's party made tension grip him, as if it had just happened. His stomach heaved nastily. "I knew him way back," he said. "In my crazy partying days, before I joined the service. I only went there as a favor for a friend."

"Ah," she murmured. "Why am I not surprised?"

"Excuse me? What the hell is that supposed to mean?"

"Nothing bad," she assured him. "By no means. It's just that helping people seems to be how you roll. It comes naturally to you."

"My friend Raisa heard that her sister Leticia had gone to that party," he told her. "She's been in some trouble already, and Raisa got nervous. Leticia wasn't answering her phone, and Raisa panicked. She knew I knew Sobel. So she begged me to go to his party and check up on her."

"Did you find Leticia?"

He shook his head.

"Ah." Jenna cocked her head to the side, frowning. "That's strange."

"Yes, it was," he agreed. "The whole thing stank."

"Did you find out if she was ever there?"

"Leticia said afterward that she was somewhere else entirely. She never even knew about that party. Someone was just winding Raisa up. For no reason she can figure out."

"What happened after they took those pictures?" Jenna asked. "You just left?"

He put his beer down, fighting the nausea. That sickening perfume stench filled his nose, even though he knew it was just a memory. Cold sweat broke out on his back. He couldn't seem to breathe. His heart was pounding triple time.

"Could we not talk about this anymore?" he said abruptly. "It wasn't my finest moment."

Jenna looked taken aback. "Sorry. Didn't mean to pry. Won't mention it again."

Damn. He'd screwed up again. "Sorry," he said. "I just—"

From the back room, someone with a mic announced the next set. Drew was grateful for the distraction. "We better get in there."

"Sure, but one second. Let me do something first." Jenna took her cocktail napkin, pressed one of her ice cubes against it and swabbed his cheek gently. "Cherise left a big red lipstick stamp on your cheek when she kissed you. Can't let another woman put her mark on my man."

The Jenna effect zapped through him at her touch, even through the cold, soggy cocktail napkin. "You're just telling me about this lipstick stamp now?" he complained. "You just let me walk around in here like that?"

"Sorry." She looked like she was trying not to smile. "Let's go listen to Roddy, now that you're decent."

Decent, ha. Drew followed her closely through the crowd as they made their way through the various rooms and toward the stage. Little did she know.

In his current state, he felt anything but decent.

Twelve

The room was packed, the band was hot and Roddy was excellent. He had loads of furious, hardcore energy, but he could be low-key and subtle when the music called for it, and he meshed with the seasoned local band as if they'd been playing together for years.

The great music and the margarita had slowly unknotted Jenna's twisted nerves. Her heart was full to overflowing as she watched Roddy play. It was a huge personal victory for her that Roddy had regained enough dexterity and flexibility with his arm to let his musical talent flow through it. That was a kiss of grace from on high. Same with Cherise's promising news about design school. The world was filled with sorrow and disaster and infamy, but tonight, she got to chalk up a few points for the good guys.

Roddy faded out expertly at the end of a song with

a shimmery tinkle of the hi-hat, and the lead singer of the band grabbed the mic.

"Boys and girls, I have been informed by our amazing guest drummer, Roddy Hepner, that we have a pair of lovebirds in the audience, and he wants to dedicate one of his own original songs to them. You lucky folks are the first to hear the Vicious Rumors perform this song, but you won't be the last. So here it is, folks! 'Thirsting for You,' written and performed by Roddy Hepner! Make space in the middle of the dance floor, everybody, and give it up for our lucky lovers… Jenna… and… Drew!"

People surged and shifted, leaving a big open space around them. They stood together, ringed by a crowd of onlookers, and the light guy trained a rose-tinted spotlight right on them. Their eyes met, as the opening chords of Roddy's beautiful ballad began.

Drew had that look on his face. Like she was the only woman in the world, and he was desperate with longing for her and her alone. His arms encircled her, pulling her close. It felt so right. So natural and inevitable.

Roddy leaned into the mic angled over the drum set and began to sing. His singing voice was wonderful. Deep and slightly rough but beautifully resonant.

The desert dust is in my shoes.
A thread of hope to see me through.
I seek what's good, I seek what's true.
But now I see I thirst for you.

It was too much. She couldn't resist the pulsing music, the intense emotions. Drew's magnetism. The look in his beautiful eyes, deep and endless as the ocean.

She tried to remind herself that she was just a normal woman, not a glammed-up movie star beauty. No way could she hold this guy's interest in the long run, or fit into his jet-setting lifestyle. She was miles out of her league. Cruising for disaster and heartbreak.

And yet, she clung to him. Their bodies had their own merged magnetism. They were one single sway-ing entity, and they were on the brink of something momentous, and unbearably sweet. Patterns of colored lights swirled and blended over the dance floor like a dreamy kaleidoscope as Roddy sang on, his voice a ten-der, scratchy croon.

My eyes are burning and my throat is dry.
My thirsty heart's been seeking far and wide.
But shining from your deep and honest eyes.
I find my reason why.

Drew cupped the back of her head in his warm hand, sliding his fingers tenderly into her hair, his gaze still locked with hers. His deep and honest eyes. They made a space just for her. They saw her so clearly. Made her feel so vibrant and alive. So real.

And they were kissing again. Nothing could have stopped it. They were floating in a shining bubble, the rest of the world shut out.

Their kiss was a language in itself, passionate and direct. It spoke of hunger and longing and tenderness, it promised exquisite pleasure, it coaxed and lured and teased.

She couldn't get enough of it. She kissed him back, saying loud and clear with the kiss everything that she'd been trying so hard not to say since the moment she met him.

Yes. God, yes. Please, yes.

She could feel his erection, hot against her belly.

She dragged him closer to feel it better, aching for his heat, his strength and energy as the song slowly ended.

The applause was thunderous. Hoots and howls from the crowd finally penetrated their magic bubble as the space around them dissolved.

People flooded back onto the dance floor, crowding in around them.

Jenna stared at Drew, willing her arms to loosen from their desperate, clinging hold, but they were not obeying her commands.

She finally managed it. By force, she pushed herself back, almost stumbling into someone behind her. Drew caught her and steadied her.

Careful. I got you. She saw his lips form the words, but couldn't hear his voice in the noise. Those beautiful lips that had just kissed her into a wanton frenzy of desire right in front of a cheering crowd.

"I have to go," she said inanely, pulling away.

His grip tightened, and his lips moved again in the raucous noise. "Where?"

"Uh…uh…the bathroom. Going to the ladies'. See you in a minute. Bye."

She pulled away again. Drew hung on for a split second, sensing her panic, but then let her go.

Jenna slipped away, weaving swiftly through the crowd and toward the door.

Someone stepped in front of her as she made for it. She ran right into him.

"Sorry, Jenna! Didn't mean to bump you!"

It was Ernest, Ava's eager-beaver young assistant, with his spiky white blond hair and his big round glasses that made him look like a crazed steam-punk aviator.

"Ernest," she said. "What on earth are you doing here?"

"The usual," Ernest said, holding up a tablet. "Recording your love!"

Jenna's insides thudded two stories down. "Oh, God. Ava told you to come here?"

"She wanted me to record Roddy's gig. The romantic dance and that be-still-my-heart steaming-hot kiss was just an awesome bonus. It's gonna totally blow up online!"

"Oh, no, no, no! Ernest, do me a favor. Don't post the dance and the kiss, okay? I understand about filming Roddy, but just leave me and Drew out of it."

Ernest looked bewildered. "Why not? I thought this was the whole point!"

"It's just, um, kind of private."

"Well, duh. Of course. That's why people go for it."

"Just don't, this time," she pleaded. "Just this once. I need a breather."

"Sorry." Ernest looked anything but sorry as he lifted his tablet. "I already uploaded it to your and Drew's YouTube channel—"

"I don't have a YouTube channel!"

"Oh, but you do, and since last week, you two have already racked up twenty-one thousand followers. Let's see, I just uploaded this video of the dance and the kiss five minutes ago, and it's got…lemme see here how many views…ooh! Seven hundred and eighty-five… six…seven… It keeps going up! You guys are a hot property!"

"That's just it," Jenna wailed. "I'm not a property! Or a reality TV star! Sometimes I need to get a drink or go hear some music and have it just be for me, for God's sake!"

Ernest gazed at her, looking blank and very clouded. "Just for you? Like, what does that even mean? What do you care if people like to watch? What does it matter?"

Jenna turned her back and left before she lost her temper and smacked the guy.

The cold wind whipped her hair as she walked down the street. Her eyes stung, and her face felt hot. Her throat was tight, like a cruel little hand was squeezing it.

But she'd signed up for this insanity.

There was a taxi cruising by. She hailed it and got in, then pulled out her phone as soon as she'd given directions to the driver. Her hand was shaking as she pulled up Drew's number and texted him.

had to go. grabbed a cab. on my way home now. sorry.

A few moments later, his response appeared. wtf! seriously?

I needed to be alone. sorry. really.

Another minute passed, and his answer appeared. WHAT DID I DO

She hastened to reply. nothing. you were great. it's me. I need some space.

A long pause. Then his terse reply. understood.

Damn it. Damn this whole thing. sorry, she repeated, digging for a tissue.

me too he responded, and then after a moment. good night. stay safe.

Great. Now he was making her feel like crap by

being courteous and classy and restrained about it. Damn that guy. He made it so…flipping…*hard*.

She had to run away from him, because she knew exactly how the evening would play out if she didn't. Drew would insist on taking her home. He would insist on walking her to the top of her steps to see her to her door. He would smolder at her with those deep, beautiful eyes that promised the moon and the stars and everything between, and she would lose her mind, drag him inside and jump all over him.

If they even made it inside. She might just ravish him right there on the porch.

She was nine-tenths in love with him already. If they went to bed, that would be it.

There would be no walking this back.

Thirteen

Jenna looked spectacularly beautiful when she joined him at the top of the stairs at the Whitebriar Club for their big entrance. It hit him like a blow.

She wore no glasses tonight. He'd barely recognized her for a moment, since her cat-eye specs were such a distinctive part of her look. She was gorgeous without them, too, in sea-foam green silk, with a string of iridescent beads as shoulder straps and shimmering beadwork on the neckline. The silk skimmed her gorgeous figure and showed a tantalizing shadow between her breasts. A hairdresser had tried to tame the curls into a decorous updo, but the efforts were in vain. The curls would not be contained. Some longer ones had sprung free already. Others swung and bounced around her delicate jaw.

She smiled at him, but her gaze dropped, embarrassed, as he took her slender arm.

"You look stunning," he said.

"Thank you."

"This isn't the black-and-white dress you talked about. Did you shop for that gown with Ava? I remember you two arguing about it a few days ago."

"Are you asking if you paid for it?" Her eyes met him with a glint of challenge. "You did not. This is one battle with your sister that I actually won, I'm proud to say. I bought this dress months ago, all by myself at a vintage clothing shop downtown. I had to get the beading restored by a costume expert, but I loved the color."

Her in-your-face tone irked him. "I was not asking if I paid for it," he said tersely. "Not that I would give a damn if I had."

She shot him a repentant look. "Sorry. I guess that sounded snarky."

"Sure as hell did," he agreed.

"I just wanted to emphasize that I am not a billionaire's plaything. Even if I do play one on TV."

"It's crystal clear to me that you're not a plaything. Don't strain yourself."

She laughed under her breath, and gave him an assessing glance. "You look sharp yourself," she said. "Nice tux."

"I do my best," he said. "You look different without your glasses."

She gave him a rueful smile. "I've always had these contacts. I'm just too lazy to use them, and they make my eyes tired and red."

"You look great both ways," he said.

"It's a classic fantasy, you know," she said. "Woman takes off glasses. Man notices for the first time that she's female."

Drew looked her up and down. "I noticed it before."

Her gaze whipped away and her color rose as they started descending the stairs toward the sea of people below. Drew was frustrated and angry with himself. When he spoke to her, every damn thing that came out of his mouth sounded like a come-on.

Solution A: Shut up and ignore her. Solution B: Avoid her altogether. As in, definitively and forever, by getting the hell out of Maddox Hill. Those were his options.

She glowed like a pearl. His arm was buzzing from that light contact with her hand, even through his tux jacket and shirt.

Enough. This farce ended tonight. It was making him miserable. That night at the Wild Side had been the last straw. Passionately kissing her while slow dancing and then having her run out on him—it was the ultimate slap.

He wasn't coming back for more. He regretted the embarrassment that breaking their false engagement would cause, but at least Jenna wouldn't have to fend off his unwelcome moves. Since he couldn't seem to stop himself from making them.

He'd get through tonight, hopefully without incident, and make the announcement to everyone concerned before he went home, and that would be that. On to the next thing.

He'd met Vann and Zack last night for a beer, to give them a heads-up before he tendered that letter of resignation he was still carrying around. His friends were angry at him. They thought he was bailing on them. He couldn't make them understand that this was a desperate survival move. A last-ditch effort to salvage what was left of his dignity.

Vann looked up from the bottom of the stairs, a frown between his dark eyes, and glanced at Jenna. His brows went up in silent question. Because of *her*?

Drew kept his face stony. As he and Jenna reached the bottom of the stairs, he saw Harold bearing down on them, a woman on his arm. She was a tall brunette with a black sequined gown and glitter spray on her prominent, bulging breasts, and she was staring straight at him.

Wait. Whoa. He knew that woman. That was Lydia, an architect he'd met in San Francisco, while working on the Magnolia Plaza project. They'd had a casual affair, but he hadn't called her since leaving San Francisco six months ago.

Or thought of her at all, to be perfectly honest.

Harold steered his date so that Lydia and he were right in front of Drew and Jenna at the foot of the stairs, blocking any further progress into the room.

Then it hit him, like a freight train. Lydia's perfume. A heavy, reeking cloud of it.

The same heinous stuff that had been squirted into his face at Sobel's party. Drew's stomach turned and he broke out in a cold sweat. Heart racing. Blood pressure dropping.

"Hi, Drew," Lydia cooed. "Looking good, as always. You've been busy, hmm?"

For a moment, Drew couldn't speak, he was fighting so hard for control. "Hello, Lydia," he forced out. "This is Jenna Somers. My fiancée."

"She knows about your fiancée," Harold said. "At least, she sure knows now."

"Yes, it's so funny how I had absolutely no clue that you'd gotten engaged to this woman last spring when you were down in San Francisco," Lydia said, in a voice that carried far and wide. "You didn't act like a man who'd just found the love of his life, as I very clearly recall." She looked Jenna over, and clucked her tongue. "Sneaky Drew."

"Excuse us. We have to go work the crowd." Drew ground the words out, pulling Jenna away from them.

"We'll talk more later! We're seated right next to each other at the banquet," Harold called after them with barely concealed glee. "You and Lydia can catch up on old times! Lydia can get to know Jenna. Won't that be nice?"

Drew pressed on, putting space between them so he could breathe, but now that the memory was activated, that horrific perfume was all he could smell, and the room was wavering in his vision. Sounds seemed distorted, as if he'd been freshly dosed with whatever drug they'd sprayed on him at the party. A stress flashback, right now? God. He was furious at his own brain for betraying him like this. *Breathe deep. Chill. Control.*

"…matter with you? Drew? What is it? Are you sick?"

Jenna was squeezing his arm and frowning. Her eyes looked worried.

"I'm fine." He forced the words out.

"You don't look fine. Your lips are white. What the hell?"

He groped for an explanation. He finally got a whiff of Jenna's scent. Honey, wildflowers. It settled him. He got a deep breath into himself. Then another.

"I think I had some kind of an allergic reaction to Lydia's perfume." He threw out the first excuse that came to his mind, but it was actually kind of true.

"I think I've got you beat there. I had an allergic reaction to Lydia herself," Jenna said with feeling. "She and your cousin are quite the poisonous pair. Better now?"

"Better," he said.

Damn good thing, too, because now they were in the room where the architectural exhibits were displayed, and the crowd closed around them. The work of the evening began; the shaking of hands, hugs and air kisses, pleasantries and chitchat, posing for photos and selfies, speaking authoritatively about the projects he'd designed. Architects and engineers, board members, local politicians and businesspeople, journalists, a stream of people to interact with. He tried to fake normal, and when he faltered, Jenna covered for him as best she could.

It felt like forever, but eventually the crowd started drifting into the stately banquet room where dinner would be served and the endless speechifying would begin. By the time they got to their table, everyone else was seated, and there was no graceful way to switch out their places elsewhere without drawing a great deal of attention to themselves.

Harold and Lydia were lying in wait for them. They both stared at Drew and Jenna from the table with cold, watchful eyes. Lydia's perfume hit his nose like a foul cloud of toxic gas. The place card with his name was right next to Lydia's chair. His guts lurched.

Jenna elbowed him to the other side and sat down next to Lydia herself, giving the other woman a big smile. "Hope you two are having a lovely evening."

"Getting better all the time." Harold's eyes dropped to Jenna's chest, where it stayed like it had been nailed there, all the way through the appetizers and the first course. Drew wanted to smack Harold under the chin until his jaws clacked together to get him to look up into Jenna's eyes when he spoke to her. Disrespectful sleaze.

Drew braved Lydia's perfume and leaned closer, careful not to inhale, to focus on what his cousin was saying.

"…on YouTube. You know, the incendiary kiss. The slow dance at the Wild Side."

"Oh, God." Jenna sounded embarrassed. "That was so silly. Ava's assistant, Ernest, was filming the drummer. We had no idea he was there. So embarrassing."

Harold took a swig of his wine and licked his lips. "So spontaneous," he commented.

"Are you usually such a shameless exhibitionist?" Lydia's eyes glittered. She had a lipstick stain on her teeth. "Does Drew inspire you? I don't blame you. That man is inspiring. No one knows that better than me. He can get a girl to do any wild, crazy thing he wants. Like, anything."

"Excuse me," Jenna said, recoiling slightly. "I'm not sure I understand."

"We just wondered." Harold gave her a lascivious smile. "You know, if the two of you get off on having the whole world watch while you, ah…get busy. Is that your thing?"

Drew shot to his feet, hitting the table. His chair fell backward, silverware rattled, a wineglass toppled. Wine splattered across the table and Lydia jumped up, scooting backward in an attempt to save her dress.

"Clumsy jerk!" she hissed. "Watch it!"

Drew ignored her, addressing his cousin. "What the hell kind of question is that?"

Harold's smile widened. The room fell silent. Everyone was watching and listening.

"I'm surprised you even heard me, you're so zoned out tonight." Harold's voice was clear and carrying. "Go easy on that wine, Drew. Are you on antihistamines? Or maybe something stronger?"

"I heard what you said," Drew said. "Do not speak to her again."

"Just admiring your fiancée," Harold said innocently. "You've smeared your red-hot scorching love affair far and wide all over the internet, so I could hardly avoid admiring her if I wanted to. Don't go all caveman on me now. It's unbecoming."

"Admire someone else. Keep your goddamn opinions to yourself."

"Drew!" Jenna said in a fierce whisper. "Holy crap! Calm down!"

Harold lifted his hands, grinning widely. "Take it easy, big guy."

"What the hell is going on?" Uncle Malcolm's furious voice came from behind him.

"Oh, no biggie." Harold's tone was light. "Just the usual. Drew's had a few too many, and now he's making a public spectacle of himself. Same old same old."

"What's this?" Uncle Malcolm glared at Drew. "What's this? Is this true?"

Drew opened his mouth, but Lydia spoke up first.

"I can't take any more of this," she quavered, clutching the wine-stained napkin she'd used to clean up her dress in her shaking hand. "You lying, cheating son of a bitch. They say you were engaged to this woman last year, when you were in San Francisco!" She pointed at Jenna. "Engaged! And you never said a word about it, all those times when you were nailing me right on the desk in your office! You filthy, selfish *bastard*!"

Gasps and low murmurs of scandalized conversation followed that outburst. The waiters all around the tables froze in place, terrified, holding their trays of prime rib.

Lydia burst into tears. She hurried out of the room, weaving and bumping between tables. Sobbing, tear-blinded, but taking her toxic cloud of perfume with her, thank God.

When she was out the door, Uncle Malcolm turned back to Drew and cleared his throat. "So. Nephew. Just to be forewarned, for the sake of my heart health, are there any more of your disgruntled chippies roaming around here on the rampage tonight?"

"Not to my knowledge," Drew said.

Uncle Malcolm harrumphed and looked around, scowling. The entire room looked back, waiting for their cue. Malcolm made a disgusted sound and waved his hand. "For God's sake, finish serving the damn meat before it's stone-cold," he snarled at the waiters. He turned to Drew. "You, come with me. I need to speak to you privately. Right now."

Drew let out a slow breath. He'd reached the end of the line.

In some ways, it was for the best. His bridges were burned, so he no longer had to torture himself with doubts or second thoughts. All he could do was move forward.

He should feel relieved, but as he looked into Jenna's worried eyes, he felt like something precious had been ripped from him. Something he'd just learned how to value.

He fixed Harold with a grim stare. "If you slime her again, I will flatten you."

"Come *now*!" his uncle snapped. "You're making a spectacle of yourself!"

"Yeah, that seems to be the general theme of my life lately." He leaned down and cupped Jenna's face. "I'm sorry," he whispered to her. "Goodbye."

He kissed Jenna, slowly and intensely, with all his pent-up desperation, ignoring the rising hum of excited chatter and his uncle's furious sputtering. Because what the hell.

He had nothing left to lose.

Fourteen

Jenna watched Drew follow his uncle out of the crowded room, head up and shoulders back, like a soldier on the march. Her fingers were pressed to her tingling, just-kissed lips. She was shocked speechless. On the verge of tears.

She jumped up to follow him, and found Harold's hot, damp fingers suddenly clamped around her wrist. "Jenna, no," he murmured. "Let them go. Sit down."

She jerked her wrist away. "With you? Why the hell should I do that?"

"Calm down," Harold said. "I am not the bad guy here."

She laughed right in his face. "You expect me to believe that?"

"This is old stuff, Jenna. Family stuff. A long time coming. Don't mix yourself up in it. You don't know the history."

She stared at Harold. "I don't think I need to. It's very clear to me."

And it was getting clearer all the time, like watching a photograph take form in a bath of darkroom chemicals. She thought of her first flash-assessment of Harold when she met him at the restaurant. Perfectly good-looking in his own right, but he suffered in comparison with Drew.

From what Ava had said, the same held true for Harold's professional life. He was competent and successful in his field, unless Drew was next to him with all of the medals and prizes and honors and high-profile projects. Next to Drew, Harold got bumped several notches down the scale, until he registered as barely higher than average.

She disliked the very thought in itself, because she did not believe in judging people in that way. But the rest of the world did.

Harold had spent his whole life in Drew's shadow and he was sick of it.

"You set him up," she said. "You sneaky bastard. You organized this whole thing."

Harold sipped his wine. "You'd like to have me be the villain so that your perfect, fantasy Drew can be innocent. News flash. He's not. Sorry to break it to you, honey."

"I am not your honey," she said. "You brought that woman up from San Francisco on purpose. I bet you told her to make that big scene as soon as Malcolm was in earshot."

"I didn't have to tell her a thing. Everything she said was literally true. Drew gets into trouble all by himself. He doesn't need help from me or anyone. Like that orgy at the Sobel party. He did that all by himself, and he does it often. That time, he just happened to get busted."

"He was lured into a trap," she said. "He was there to help a friend."

"That's what he told you?" Harold gave her a pity-ing look. "I checked the dates of your Women in STEM speech in San Francisco last year, when you and Drew hooked up. I know for a fact that Drew was screwing Lydia that whole time, and for months afterward. You were sharing him back then, Jenna. Knowing Drew, you're probably sharing him now. He's a star, and he never denies himself. I'm sorry to hurt you, but it's true. Think long and hard before you get in too deep with him."

Jenna stepped back, whipping her arm away before Harold could grab her wrist again. To hell with this guy. He wasn't worth another moment of her time.

And she had a few choice things she wanted to say to Malcolm Maddox.

She marched through the tables, chin high, ignoring the muttering and the stares, following the path Drew and his uncle had taken. Once outside the ballroom, she homed in on Malcolm's haranguing voice. It came from upstairs, so she followed it up, and down the wide hall until she came to the double doors of the Cedar Salon, a luxurious old-fashioned parlor.

As she threw the doors open, the old man's voice blared even louder.

"...sick of your depraved antics! After all Hendrick's complaining about your behavior, you decide to put on a floor show like that right in front of all of them?"

"Uncle, I didn't plan on that woman showing up to—"

"You think you dodged a bullet when you trotted

out your perfect little Miss Butter-Wouldn't-Melt-In-Her-Mouth, eh? You think you can use her like some sort of goddamn human shield. But whatever you think you might have gained by that cheap trick, you just lost ten times over, and I for one am not fooled by your—"

"He is not using me!" Jenna yelled. "If anything, I'm the one using him!"

Malcolm's head whipped around, eyes shocked. "This is a private conversation, Miss Somers!"

"I don't care. If you're trash-talking me, I insist on participating. Miss Butter-Wouldn't-Melt-In-Her-Mouth, my ass! You should be ashamed of yourself!"

Malcolm Maddox stared at her for a moment, mouth open, and cleared his throat. "Well," he said gruffly. "That is a matter of opinion."

"So now you know my opinion!"

"Certainly. At that volume, the whole building knows your opinion."

"I'm fine with that," she said hotly. "I have nothing to hide. Nothing."

"That's not the case for him, unfortunately." Malcolm gestured at Drew. "You heard what that woman said. It's the story of his life! Is that what you want for yourself?"

"He was set up! He goes miles out of his way to help people, time and time again. He took a bullet in Iraq, risking his life for his country. Does none of that count for you?"

"Oh, God." Drew looked pained. "Jenna, I don't need for you to—"

"You just hush up!" She rounded on him furiously. "You've been doing a crap job at defending yourself lately, so step aside and let me handle it this time!"

"I appreciate your zeal, young lady," Malcolm said. "But you're sticking your nose into matters that aren't your business."

"Guilty as charged," she said. "I don't give a damn. Just don't expect me to smile and nod while someone I care about is being put down. I just…won't…do it. Period."

Malcolm Maddox frowned at her for a moment, then his gaze flicked to Drew. "Hmph," he grunted. "Played the wounded soldier card, eh?"

"I play the cards I have," Drew said.

"Don't blame you, to be honest." Malcolm looked her over, his eyes sharp and assessing. "She is something when she gets going, hmm?"

"That she is," Drew agreed.

"Do not talk about me as if I'm not here," Jenna snapped.

Malcolm laughed and gestured toward Jenna with his cane. "Hang on to this one if you can, boy," he said gruffly. "But you know damn well you don't deserve her. You're just a dog on the furniture. Pull yourself together. Try not to make spectacles of yourselves for the rest of the evening, if you can possibly manage it, eh? Both of you."

He turned his back and stumped out, hunched over his cane, still muttering.

Drew and Jenna looked at each other after the door fell to after him. Jenna shook her head, bewildered. "Um… What just happened?"

"Looks like you just charmed Uncle Malcolm," Drew said. "Congratulations."

She stared at him. "Charmed him? By scolding him? *That's* what charms him?"

"We're a contrary bunch." Drew's tone was almost apologetic. "And he favors strong women. With strong opinions."

"Oh, God." Jenna pressed both hands to her hot cheeks. "This is so crazy." She started digging in her evening bag for a tissue, sniffling into it.

"What's wrong?" Drew asked. "Why are you crying?"

"It happens when I lose my temper. Something shorts out in my brain. Don't be alarmed, you don't have to comfort me or anything like that. It'll pass quickly."

Drew still looked worried. "You're sure you're okay?"

"Fine," she assured him. "Really."

He just looked at her, hesitating. "Ah…thanks," he said, awkwardly.

"For what?"

"For coming out swinging like that. For having my back. I know that it was part of the whole being-engaged act, and I think we can hang that masquerade up at this point. But act or no act, it felt really good to hear."

She was horrified by a fresh wave of tears. "Oh, crap," she muttered. "That was not an act, Drew Maddox." There it was. The truth. She'd blurted it out at last.

His eyes sharpened. "Meaning what? You haven't been pretending?"

"Not at all," she admitted. "I've been a goner ever since I dumped that pitcher of sangria on you. I know I shouldn't tell you this, but that's the short circuit in my brain. I cry, and then I blurt out stuff people don't necessarily want to hear. Anyhow. I've done enough damage tonight, so I think I'll just get my coat and get the hell out of—"

She let out a startled squeak as Drew pulled her against himself and kissed her.

It was electrifying. His breathless urgency. His hard body, muscles taut, shaking with emotion. The shining thrill racing through her, the ache of hunger in her body, always a constant smolder, but when he touched her, it flared into a bonfire.

Jenna wrapped her arms around his neck and melted into him. Kissed him back with everything she had. Ravenous for the delicious heat of his mouth as a new world of emotions and sensations opened up inside her.

Drew maneuvered them down onto an antique love seat, pulling her down onto his lap and kissing her bare shoulder with desperate tenderness. The beaded straps of the dress slid down, and the top of the lacy cups of her strapless bra were showing. Drew made a rough, tormented sound in his throat and pressed his face against them. Both of them moaned at the sweetness of it. The warm tenderness of his lips was an intoxicating sensation, kissing her, nuzzling her. His arms were so strong. Everywhere he touched her touched off a rush of delight. He stroked her back.

"Oh, God. So hot and soft," he murmured. "So smooth. You're killing me."

She settled right over that hard, unyielding bulge of his erection and leaned down to kiss him again. The bodice of the dress was slipping down but his hands stroking her bare back felt so good, and his hot kiss was so searching and seductive.

The doors squeaked, and a swell of noise behind them made them both freeze and turn. Drew's body went tense beneath her.

Uncle Malcolm, Hendrick, Bev, Harold, Ava, Ernest,

eyes popping, mouths agape, and a dozen more people stood right behind them, pushing, craning. On tiptoe. A hum of shocked murmurs, embarrassed giggles.

"Oh, my God." Jenna struggled with her neckline, tugging it back up over the cups of her strapless bra before sliding off Drew's lap and onto her feet.

"Out! Everyone get out!" Uncle Malcolm shouted, but there was no possible retreat for the people in the doorway. The crush of gawkers pressing up behind them blocked their escape. Harold's face was a cold mask. Ava's smile was conspiratorial. Like she was in on the joke.

Except it wasn't a joke. It never really had been.

Bev smirked at her husband. "Well, Hendrick, that looks pretty sincere to me, wouldn't you say? I think I won this bet. Better get ready to pay up."

Hendrick just peered at them, his thick eyebrows knitted together like he just couldn't figure out what was going on.

Not that Jenna was doing much better, when it came right down to it.

"Get back!" Malcolm bawled. "All of you! Out! Damn it!"

Jenna finally got her dress straightened and slid her shoe back on. She scooped up her beaded evening bag from where it had fallen on the carpet. "That's my cue," she murmured to Drew. "Time to disappear."

"With me," Drew said swiftly. "Only with me."

She looked into his eyes, and promptly forgot that people were watching them. The longing in his eyes called out to her, a sweet pull so strong, not even public humiliation could quench it. It just raged on and on, wanting what it wanted.

"Yes," she said. "Let's disappear together."

His eyes flashed, and his warm hand closed around hers.

Malcolm overheard them. "That would be best, since neither one of you seems to be capable of any self-control," he snarled. "For the love of God, go! Let me try to salvage what's left of my company's image."

"Don't be grumpy, Uncle." Ava was still trying not to smile. "Everyone loves it, and you know it."

"Enough, Av," Drew said. "Dial it down to zero."

"Me?" Ava's chin rose. "I'm not dialing anything. I'm not doing a damn thing, bro. You two are doing it all on your own. But it would be a shame to stop now when everyone's having so much fun, don't you think?"

"We're out of here." Drew slid his arm around Jenna's waist and made for the crowd of people who blocked the doors. "Make way."

The steely quality in his voice made people actually shuffle backward. Jenna's face burned as they forced their way through, but Harold's cold eyes chilled her as she passed. She could feel the anger emanating from him.

People tried to speak to them, but she couldn't follow what they were saying. Drew ignored them, sweeping them both onward through the press of people and down the stairs, toward the coat check desk. He helped her slip her coat on. "You're shaking," he said as they made their way toward the exit. "Put on my coat. It's heavier."

"Not from the cold. I'm actually kind of hot," she said, as they went out the door.

The cold, damp night air felt good against her feverish face.

"Where's your car?" he asked.

"Didn't bring it," she told him, teeth still chattering. "I used a car service. Didn't want to be bothered with parking or driving."

"Good," he said, as the parking attendant pulled up in his silver Jag.

He opened the door for her, and she got in, waiting while he tipped the attendant and got in himself. Then they sat in stunned silence for a moment.

She laughed shakily. "Holy cow. What a circus."

"Yes it was." He started the engine and pulled out onto the street. "I'm sorry to put you through that."

"It wasn't your fault. I mouthed off to your uncle. I showed my strapless bra to the Board of Directors and God knows who all else. That's going to follow me around until I die."

He laughed. "At least the bra was still on."

"Well, thank God for that," she said. "I can't believe how I just behaved. I can't carry on in public like that. I'm going to lose all my professional credibility."

"I'm sorry if I put you in a compromising position," he said. "The last thing I want is to damage you professionally."

Jenna wound the beaded strap of her purse around her fingers. "I imagine that whole exhibition was kind of a buzzkill for you, right?"

"No." Drew reached across the console and grabbed her hand without taking his eyes off the road.

The contact with his hand flashed up her arm, then raced instantly to deeper, more secret places. "No?" She tried to keep her voice even, but it still quavered, betraying her. "You're not traumatized?"

"I barely noticed them," he admitted. "All I saw in

that room was you. Nothing on earth could kill my buzz."

A glow of anticipation was filling her whole body.

"How about you?" he asked. "Are you still with me?"

She squeezed his hand. "Oh, yeah."

He squeezed back. "Can I take you to my house? It's closer. And I want you to see it."

"Yes, please. I'd like that."

Game on. She was done trying to control this.

Whatever he offered, she would take. If it was just his body, that was fine. Just a fling, fine. Just one night, also fine. She wanted this. She was grabbing it with both hands.

She could process the hurt later. There would be plenty of time for that.

Wow. Just look at her. After all her lofty notions and uppity attitude, she'd tumbled into Drew's honeyed trap after all.

She had just officially become a billionaire's plaything.

So be it. It was finally time to play.

Fifteen

Drew was tongue-tied the entire way home. Having Jenna in his car, taking her to his home—it was huge. It filled up his chest until he could barely breathe, let alone speak. He'd never felt this way, even when he was a teenager just learning about sex. He'd started out by faking it. Pretending to be cool and confident and smooth until that became the truth.

But it wasn't his truth anymore. Not with Jenna. He couldn't pretend. All bets were off with her. Nothing could be taken for granted. And the stakes were so damn high.

He kept his grip on her slim, cool hand, when he didn't need his own hand for driving. Whenever he had to let go of her, he promptly reached for her again. Assuring himself that she was real.

But she was also nervous. He could not screw this up.

He pulled into the driveway that led to his property on Lake Washington and parked the car in the garage.

"You designed this house," she said.

"How did you know that?"

"I've seen your buildings. I knew it was yours because it was so different from the lakeside McMansions we passed. Your designs don't fight with their environment. They're harmonious."

He was absurdly pleased that she got it, and that she liked the house he'd designed for himself. As well as embarrassed. He was showing off to impress her, like a little kid.

"Come on in." He took her hand to lead her down the flagstone path that wound through the trees and landscaped garden of the front lawn to the main entrance. When they went inside, Jenna stood in the middle of the entry hall with its row of skylights, and then strolled into the living room. A long wall of glass overlooked the lake, with lights from the other side of Lake Washington wavering on the water. French doors led out onto the patio. A wooden walkway wound through the grass and trees down to a floating dock, and his boat. Another thing he'd been too busy to use lately.

"I'll give you a tour tomorrow," he offered. "When we have some light."

But not now. I'm dying to touch you.

"Okay," she murmured.

Drew watched her as she wandered around his living room. He tried to remember what common courtesy demanded.

"Can I take your coat?" He slid open the panels in the wall in the entry hall, revealing the deep cedar-lined closet. She moved closer, turning to let him lift the coat from her shoulders. That released an intoxicating waft of sweet fragrance. Her hair had rebelled from its coif, her ringlets floating up free and dangling around her throat. Her skin was so fine. So soft. He wanted to bury his face against it.

He swallowed, hard. "Can I get you a drink? I have whiskey, brandy, or I could open a bottle of wine. Or mix you a drink from the bar. Anything you like."

She peeked over her shoulder, a seductive smile curving the corners of her luscious red lips. "Better not," she murmured. "I'm in an altered state already."

"Want me to build a fire?" he asked.

"When we're already so hot?"

Her light, teasing words made the heat roar through him. His hands flexed, clenched. "You have a point," he said, rigidly controlled.

"I'm too impatient for time-wasting moves like that," she told him. "After weeks of being constantly tantalized."

He let out a harsh crack of laughter. "Me, tantalizing you? Like hell! I've been stretched out at your feet ever since that very first day. I have held nothing back!"

"And this smooth seductive patter of yours? The drink, the fire?" She rolled her eyes at him. "Are you going to show me your etchings now? Your butterfly collection?"

Her voice was playful, but he was so attuned to her now, he could sense she was wound incredibly tight. Trying to keep him at arm's length with her teasing.

The first step was to unwind her. Very…slowly.

He didn't try to reply. Just came up behind her, and leaned down to kiss her shoulder, letting his lips trail up to the nape of her neck. No words. No seductive patter. Just his lips, moving over her skin. A slow, dragging caress, the rasp of his teeth. A delicate nip. Her hair was so soft and fragrant. So warm.

She tilted her head, allowing him more access.

He took advantage of it. Gave himself up to it. Oh, yeah. He could do this all night. Hot, hungry kisses, slowing down time. Exploring every inch of her throat, her shoulders. Getting her to relax and soften in his grasp. He wanted her helpless with pleasure. So aroused, she couldn't even stand up. That was the goal.

Her breath was uneven as he slid his arms around her waist from behind. One hand splayed over her belly, whisper-thin silk separating him from her warm skin. He loved the tremor in her body, the breathless sound in the back of her throat as he slid his hand up, feeling her rib cage. The soft weight of her breasts. The smoothness of her skin above the dress. Her racing pulse.

Jenna placed her hands over his. Not stopping them, just covering them. Pressing them closer to her. He leaned down, kissing her shoulders. Nudging the beaded strap of her gown until it fell off one shoulder. Then the other. He was slow. Persistent.

His pulsing erection was pressed up to her backside, and she leaned back against him, welcoming the contact. Inviting his touch, with that dreamy smile on her face.

It was getting more and more difficult to keep this slow. His hands shook, but he soldiered on. He found a stray hairpin trapped in one of her ringlets during his nuzzling kisses, so he took a moment to sort through her hair and pull out all the pins, setting that halo of wild ringlets loose. "I like it best when it's like this," he said. "Free and wild."

"Getting wilder by the second," she murmured. "The way you kiss me makes me crazy."

"That's how I want you to feel," he said. "I want you primed."

"That's how I want you, too."

"Not an issue. Done deal. I've been in that primed state pretty much since you first kissed me in the elevator."

She looked back at him, the mix of colors in her eyes hypnotically beautiful. Then she straightened up and turned around to face him, shrugging the bodice of her dress down until it was hanging off her hips.

She shook back her hair, holding his gaze with a blaze of sexy challenge in her eyes as she reached behind herself and undid the clasp of her bra.

She let it drop, and stood there, shoulders back. Displaying herself. The color in her cheeks was high. Her lips parted, breath coming fast. But her hands still shook.

Her breasts were so beautiful. High, full and soft, with tight dark pink nipples, and her skin was so fine-grained and smooth and perfect. The chill in his house had given her goose bumps but her chest had a pink blush that matched the one on her cheeks.

He wanted to lunge for her like a ravenous animal. *Easy does it.*

Drew placed his hands on her waist. A tremor went through her at the contact, then another as his hands slid slowly upward, over her rib cage. Under her arms.

He cupped her breasts, almost reverently. "You are spectacular."

"I'm still waiting for the spectacle to begin. You certainly do keep a girl waiting."

"I'm trying not to rush it," he said. "We'll never get this first time back. I want the memory to be perfect."

Her smile sent fire shooting through every part of his body. "Really? Wow. I had no idea you were so sentimental."

"Neither did I," he admitted. "That thought has never passed through my mind before in my life. Only with you."

Her eyebrows went up. "Well, then," she murmured. "I am honored to be the one to have sparked an original thought in your head."

He gave her a narrow look. "I'm not sure quite how to take that."

She laughed at him. "You don't have to take it at all. I'm just messing with you." She reached up to deftly loosen his bow tie, then she started in on the buttons of his shirt, sliding her hand inside to caress his chest. "The way I feel right now, we couldn't make anything but amazing memories. Relax. Let yourself go. I trust you."

He knew she was just talking about sex, but the rush of emotion her words gave him made him throb and burn. Her hands moved over his chest.

"Just one quick thing first," she said hesitantly. "I don't carry condoms around in my evening bag, so…"

"I have some," he assured her.

"Good. That's a relief. But since we're on the subject, let's just power through this part all at once. I got myself tested for everything under the sun a few weeks ago, after I found out that Rupert was cheating on me.

Thank God he didn't give me anything. I'm in the clear, just so you know."

"Thanks for bringing it up. Me, too. Just got tested myself, and I'm all good."

"Excellent," she said, undoing another button, and then another, spreading his shirt and murmuring in approval at what she found. "In that case. I have a contraceptive implant. So… We could just dispense with the latex. If you'd like."

Liked? The idea of no latex with Jenna made him dizzy. "Dream come true."

"Great," she murmured, leaning forward to kiss his chest. "So… Do you mean to do the deed right here in your foyer? I wouldn't mind, since it's all so beautiful—"

He scooped her up into his arms. She made a startled sound. "Whoa! The hell?"

He carried her down the long corridor, toward his bedroom. "My bedroom."

She wound her fingers into the fabric of his shirt collar and tugged it. "Wow," she whispered. "How masterful and ravishing of you."

"Do you go for that?"

"Sure, if it's you."

Good. He nudged the door to the master bedroom open with his foot. His bedroom was very large and sparsely furnished, everything in it subservient to the view. Two enormous windows looked out over Lake Washington, the waving trees and garden. The light filtering in from outside was just enough to make the bamboo floor planks gleam and dimly illuminate the low, enormous bed.

Drew carried Jenna over to the bed and laid her

down, climbing on top of her. Covering her slender body with his own.

She said she trusted him to let himself go, and he was taking her at her word.

Sixteen

She felt like a live flame. Pure and essential, like everything superfluous had gone up in smoke. She barely recognized the woman moving beneath Drew, making those helpless gasping sounds. Enthralled by him, and yet more marvelously free than she'd ever felt.

She loved his heat, his lithe, solid body on top of her. His bare chest pressed to her breasts. Then he slid farther down, kissing her throat, then her collarbone.

When he got to her breasts, she floated up to a new level of shining hyperawareness. She clutched his head, fingers slipping through his short hair, thighs squeezing together, just trying to breathe. She wanted to wrap her legs around him, but her thighs were clamped between his, leaving her writhing, gasping, struggling instinctively toward release as her excitement crested to terrifying heights—and crashed down on her.

The climax pulsed through her body. Deep throbs of pleasure wiped her out.

When she opened her eyes, Drew was poised over her, his eyes hot and fascinated.

"I'd call that a good beginning," he said. "I love watching you come."

She wanted to laugh, but she was so limp, her chest barely lifted against his weight. But he still felt it, rolling off her and pulling her tight against him, so they were on their sides facing each other.

She plucked at his shirt. "Get that off," she said. "I want the full effect."

Drew sat up, shrugging off the tux jacket, wrenching off the shirt. He tossed it away, prying off shoes and socks while he was at it.

Jenna sat up, too, with some effort, as relaxed as she felt, and sat on the bed, struggling with the ridiculously tiny buckles on the ankle straps of her shoes. It was almost impossible, with fingers that were still shaking.

Drew sank down to his knees on the floor in front of her. His big, warm hands pushed hers away. "Let me."

He undid the buckles swiftly, tossing the shoes behind him, and looked into her eyes as he slid his big, warm hands up the outside of her legs, all the way up to the bands of stretchy lace that held up her thigh-high stockings, and then onto the warm, bare skin above them. He began exploring, with his usual hypnotically slow, magical caresses.

"The dress has got to go," he said. "But leave the stockings on."

She stood up, grabbing his shoulder to steady herself, and almost couldn't get a good grip, it was so thick with muscle. "I just got all that fancy beading repaired," she murmured. "Don't want to tear out the seams."

Drew tugged the crumpled pale green fabric gently down over her hips, until it fell to the floor. He made a low, grinding sound deep in his throat as he swayed forward, pressing his face to her belly.

His breath was so hot, so tender. His lips trailed over her skin, and left a glowing trail of hyper-sensitized erogenous zone every place he touched.

She slid her fingers into his hair, caressing his ears, his cheekbone, his jaw. Savoring the texture of his faint rasp of beard shadow, squeezing the massive breadth of his powerful shoulders.

Drew hooked his thumbs into the pale lace of her panties and tugged them down. She shook them off her ankle, and sucked in a startled breath as he leaned to kiss her, his mouth moving skillfully over her sensitive flesh while his hands cupped her bottom. She vibrated like a plucked string.

"So good." Drew kissed his way around the swatch of hair adorning her mound.

Jenna wanted to respond somehow, but she was beyond words. She felt so vulnerable, so naked. Incredibly female. Tormented by longing as she wound her fingers into his hair, tugging wordlessly. Demanding more, more, more.

He responded eagerly, pressing his mouth to her, caressing her tender inner folds. He was bold and generous and tireless. So incredibly good at it. He went at her with ruthless skill until she was shaking wildly, head thrown back. Keening low in her throat, completely focused on the sensual swirl of his tongue, the delicate flick, the slow, suckling pull—and she came apart, as he unleashed another wave of shuddering pleasure.

Afterward, she found herself lying down with no clear memory of how she got there, but Drew was leaning over her, pulling the billowy, puffy comforter over her.

"Good?" he asked.

She licked her lips. "I never felt anything so fabulous in my life," she whispered.

"Excellent." She couldn't read his face in the dimness, but he sounded pleased.

She grabbed his belt. "The pants need to come off. I don't want to be naked alone."

"Oh, don't worry." He shucked his pants promptly. "I'll keep you company."

He worked his briefs down, and his erection sprang free. Jenna sat up with a murmur of approval. He was stiff, flushed, ready. She closed her hand around him, and Drew covered her hand with his own, moving it up and down his thick shaft. So hot and hard and sexy. Exciting her beyond belief. She stroked him, exploring him, teasing him, squeezing him. She loved making him shudder and gasp and moan.

Finally he stopped her hands, and stretched out next to her, sliding under the covers and into her arms.

The shock of contact with her whole body made her gasp. He was scorching hot. It was overwhelming. The buzz of intense awareness felt both brand-new and incredibly familiar, like she'd known him since eternity. Their connection was timeless, inevitable, in thrall to that kiss. Tongues dancing, arms clasping, legs twining. Struggling to get closer.

She didn't know what was up, what was down. He

was her center of gravity, the only one that mattered. At some point, based on the fact that she was somewhat breathless, she realized that she was underneath, pinned by his solid weight. Her legs twined around his, pulling him closer. The heat of his erection throbbed against her belly.

"You ready?" he asked.

It was hard to respond, with her throat so soft and hot, her lips shaking. She nodded, pulling him closer. Insistently.

His grin flashed briefly in the dimness as he shifted on top of her, positioning himself as she arched and opened, stretching luxuriously.

"You're so soft," he murmured, parting her tender inner folds as he moved himself against her with small, teasing strokes.

She couldn't form words anymore, not in this state. She was stuck with nonverbal communication. She dug her nails into his chest and let out a low, breathless moan as he pushed himself slowly inside her exquisitely sensitized body. He filled her completely.

She could hardly move, but she was softer and slicker and hotter than she'd ever imagined being. They started slow, just rocking together, tiny surges, but soon it was just like all the other times he'd touched her. She felt possessed, out of control, writhing, making wild, demanding sounds, nails digging into his back. Demanding everything.

And he gave it to her. Deep, rhythmic thrusts that drove her wild, caressing all the new tender sweet spots that had suddenly come into being just for him. Every stroke was marvelous, perfect, poignant. She didn't want it to ever stop, but already the charge was building, bigger than ever before.

She had no idea what was on the other side of something so huge, just that it was unprecedented. She could burn to ash, disappear. But it didn't matter. There was no question of choice. She just let that wild power have its way. Like tumbling off a cliff.

And discovering, to her astonishment, that she could fly.

Drew lifted up onto his elbows, easing slowly and reluctantly out of her clinging depths. So hot and sweet. He hoped he'd read her cues right in his own frenzy, desperate for the next thrust before he finished the one he was doing. She was small and tight and perfect, and he hadn't kept it slow. The whole thing had gotten away from him.

He stretched out next to her, touching her body along its entire length, everywhere he could. Stroking her back and waiting. Holding his breath for the verdict.

He didn't have to wait long. Her beautiful eyes fluttered open, dazed and dilated. The smile she gave him was glowing. "Hey, you."

He pulled her hand up to his mouth, kissing her knuckles. "You good?"

"Great," she said. "I didn't know that was even possible."

"What?" He was cautiously hopeful. "Meaning…?"

"Feeling like that. Coming like that. It was… I never felt anything like it."

The tension inside him relented. "Ah. Okay. Good, then."

Her eyes went wide. "Wait," she said, rolling up to

prop her head on her hand. "Were you actually worried?"

"Just wanted it to be perfect for you," he said, kissing her hand again.

"*Perfect* is the wrong word," she told him. "*Perfect* is careful and nervous and controlled. It wasn't like that. It was wild. Magic. But you know that. You were there."

He was grinning now, helplessly. "Still am. Not going anywhere."

He kissed her, and in a heartbeat, he was stone-hard again, as needy and aching as he was before.

Too soon. He had to hang back. Take it easy.

He rolled onto his belly, and tried to content himself by stroking her warm, lithe body under the covers. Studying the beautiful planes and curves and hollows of her face and throat in the shadowy dimness. So spectacularly pretty. So unique.

"I just don't get it," he said, almost to himself.

"What's that?"

"Your ex. I don't get how he could look at anyone else when he had you."

She snorted. "He didn't see me. He just expected to be the smack-dab center of my attention at all times. My job was to constantly make him feel a certain way about himself, and I couldn't keep up with it. It was exhausting."

"He works in your field, right?"

"He's an engineer, like me," she said. "He was on the team that developed the design for Cherise's arm. I'm not angry like I was before, though. Only my pride was hurt. Everything else is intact. All things considered, it was a near miss. He and Kayleigh did me a favor. A public, embarrassing, ego-crushing favor. Very generous of them. I'm grateful."

Drew shifted in the bed, rolling her over on top of him. "And I'm glad."

"About what?" Jenna positioned herself, and her sensual wiggling felt so good.

He adjusted their position so that she was settled right exactly where he needed her. She gasped as he pulsed his hips up against her. "I'm glad you're not hung up on him," he said. "Because I don't want to share."

She looked startled. "Um. Wow."

They stared at each other for a long moment, and Jenna's expression changed, as the ever-present heat between them surged.

She placed her hands against his chest and pushed herself until she was sitting up, straddling him. Tossing the cover back so it landed on his legs. Shoulders back. Eyes on his, full of fire. Full of invitation as she reached down, caressing his stiff, aching length.

She placed her other hand on his chest. "I can feel your heart. In both places."

Drew covered her hand with his own, pressing it. Then he seized her hips, lifting her up so he could position himself beneath her. She danced over him until they got the angle right, and she let out a low, wordless moan as she took him inside, sinking down with shivering slowness into her tight, clinging heat.

Together they found the perfect surging rhythm. He was desperate to explode inside her, and he also wanted this to last forever. Every point of contact was as sweet as a deliberate kiss. He went for all of them with deep, gliding strokes. Seeking out everything that made her melt and moan, the power building in her body.

She cried out, throwing her head back, convulsing over him, and just in time because his own climax was rumbling in his head, a landslide about to come down on him. Huge and inevitable.

It overtook him. Blotted out the world.

Some unmeasurable interval of time later, they drifted back to normal consciousness together. She was draped over his chest, kissing it.

"I knew it would be good with you," she murmured. "I just had no idea how good. My imagination didn't go that far."

"Same with me," he admitted.

He was taken aback when she looked up and laughed. "Oh, please," she said. "Seriously, Drew? With your history?"

"What history is that?"

"Come on," she scoffed. "With all the famous beauties that you swan around with on the red carpets and the luxurious yachts?"

He jerked up off the pillow. "What does that have to do with anything? A lot of women have been associated with me. That doesn't mean I had satisfying relationships with them. Or great sex. Or that I felt intimate with them. That's never come easy to me. Women complain that I can't open up. But with you, I can. It's different with you."

Jenna propped her head on her arms to study him. It was as if her beautiful eyes stared straight into his mind. All that sharp intelligence focused on him, trying to distinguish truth from bullshit. Trying to decide if he was for real. He was on trial.

He stared back. "I have never felt this way," he said.

"Never. About anyone. That is not a slick, calculated line. I swear to God, I am being straight with you."

Jenna slowly reached out both hands, cupping his face, stroking it gently with her fingertips, from his cheekbones to his jaw. She gave him a misty smile, and nodded.

"Okay," she whispered. "I believe you."

It was as if the chains broke loose inside him, all at once. He pulled her close, and off they went again.

Like nothing on earth could hold them back.

Seventeen

Jenna drifted up from sleep, disoriented. She felt so good. Incredibly warm.

She opened her eyes. The two enormous windows showed the glow of sunrise on the lake and in the sky. Drew was behind her. One arm draped around her shoulders, the other curved around the pillow where she lay.

She stared at his powerful forearm, mere inches from her eyes, admiring the details. Trying to breathe. She couldn't believe this was real. It seemed like a dream, but her backside was pressed against his immense heat.

His bedroom was beautiful in the morning light. Soothing to the eye. Light reflected off the gleaming floorboards. Swaths of green and waving boughs set off the lake view. Mist rose in tendrils off the water. Tranquil and lovely.

Their hastily discarded clothing was strewn around the bed. She saw one of her shoes. Her dress, sadly crumpled. Sacrificed on the altar of lust, but she regretted nothing.

She really was here. Naked in Drew Maddox's bed. She'd spent the night in his luxurious bachelor lair. She'd been well and truly seduced.

Last night had been a revelation. Some time ago, after a series of romantic disappointments, she'd come to the conclusion that she was just one of those people for whom sex was just never going to be a big priority. She just didn't get what the fuss was about. She was a busy person. Everyone had to decide where to put their energy and attention. A family would have been nice, but all those songs about passion and obsession and need... She just didn't get it.

Well, damn. She got it now, like a wrecking ball. Roddy's song flashed through her mind.

In your deep and honest eyes, I find my reason why. Her own eyes overflowed.

No, no, no. Cool your jets, girl. Too much, too soon. She had to keep this light. She appreciated Drew's pronouncements about how special their connection was— that was all very sweet and lovely, and she meant to enjoy it to the fullest—but she wasn't diving into this headfirst. She was going to tiptoe. Eyes wide open.

She peered over at the digital clock with eyes that burned and stung from sleeping in her contacts. She had an early lunch with Bev and her friends from the Bricker Foundation. She barely had time to organize for it. And Smudge would be so hurt at being abandoned all night, he probably wouldn't speak to her for days.

She slid out of Drew's arms, trying not to disturb

him, and slipped off the bed, gathering those of her things that she could find. The bathroom was in disarray, water and towels on the floor. She'd come in at some point to wash up, but Drew had joined her and turned her shower into another delicious erotic interlude. The memory made her face go hot.

After a quickie rinse in the shower, she dried off and put on her clothes, insofar as she could. The stockings were lost in Drew's bed somewhere. Her hairpins were scattered all over his entry hall. Her bra was missing in action. She pulled on the dress without it, hoping that her landlady and the other tenants wouldn't see her waltzing up the steps to her house in the morning in rumpled evening wear. Her first official walk of shame, whoo-hoo. Better late than never.

The makeup smears were alarming. A dab of lotion she found on Drew's shelf got off the worst of it, but nothing would dim that wild feverish flush on her face.

Or the glow of terrified happiness in her eyes.

He was still asleep, stretched out on the rumpled bed, the coverlet draped across his waist, when she tiptoed out of the bathroom. She moved closer to admire, and saw the scars on his lower back that she hadn't noticed in the dark the night before. The ragged path the bullet had made as it tore through him. The more regular surgical scars that surrounded it. Her muscles tightened in cringing sympathy, imagining all that pain.

She needed to call for a ride home, and for that, she needed her phone. The evening bag was probably still in the foyer somewhere, so she tiptoed out there barefoot. There it was, on the dining room table. She scooped up as many hairpins as she could find, and shoved them into her bag. She needed to know where she was to call for a pickup, so she poked around until she found an architectural magazine with a mailing label. She made the call and was heading back for her shoes when she heard him.

"Jenna? You here?"

"I'm here," she called back. "Just getting myself together."

Drew was sitting up and leaning back against his hands, the cover draped across his lap, hiding all his excellent masculine bounty. Probably just as well. She had to avoid temptation this morning, considering her time crunch. But oh, he was so gorgeous.

He looked dismayed to see her dressed. "You're leaving already?"

"I'm so sorry, but I have to go," she said apologetically, scooping up her shoes. She sat down on the bed next to him to put them on. "I have appointments today."

"Can't you reschedule? Say you're sick. Loll around naked in bed with me here all day. I'm no master chef, but I can handle bacon, eggs and toast just fine."

It sounded so wonderful. She struggled with the stupidly tiny shoe buckle, fighting the overwhelming urge to give in and stay with him. "I'm sorry," she repeated. "It sounds great, and I'd love to, really, but I just can't. Not this time."

"Then I'll drive you home. Let me throw on some clothes."

"Oh, no, no," she said quickly. "The car service is on its way."

A guarded look came over his face. "You're not panicking on me, are you?"

"No way." She finished with the last buckle, and leaned to give him a slow, lingering kiss. "I am not blowing you off. By no means. I promise. I loved every second of last night. It was incredible."

"Then have lunch with me," he said. "After your thing."

"Lunch *is* the thing, I'm afraid. An early one, with Bev and her lady friends from the Bricker Foundation. Some of whom may have seen me wrapped around you in my bra last night, so I think I should change my clothes and freshen my makeup before I face them. Plus, I am desperate to get these contacts out and put my glasses back on."

He grinned. "I love your glasses."

She kissed him again. "Good," she said. "That is extremely lucky for you."

"Dinner, then?" he asked hopefully.

She was floating now, and couldn't even control the smile that seemed wrapped all the way around her head. "Dinner," she agreed. "We're on. Text me the details."

"Will do." He tugged the comforter off his lap, displaying his erection, in all its glory. "All the details," he agreed. "For your viewing pleasure. Nothing held back."

She looked him over appreciatively, biting her lip. "You're making this really hard, Drew," she murmured.

"I think that's my line," he said, and then cut off her giggles with a kiss that sent a fresh jolt of aching sexual hunger through her body. In no time, she was stretched out on the bed, feet dangling off, arms wound around him. Oh, that seductive bastard. Out of nowhere, she was a breath away from pulling her clothes off and leaping on him again.

But she pulled back, breath hitching, face red. *Play it cool. Keep it light.*

"You're so bad," she said, her voice unsteady. "Enticing me."

"I can't help myself. How am I supposed to make myself respectable for work with a hard-on like this?"

She shrugged. "Don't know, but I just heard my phone beep with a message, so the car is probably waiting out there. You're on your own with that dilemma. Poor you. Maybe I can help you brainstorm possible solutions for that problem tonight at dinner. If you're good."

"Cruel, heartless Jenna. I promise, I'll be good."

The car service SUV was waiting in the driveway, and the driver had a long-suffering look on his face, as if he'd been there for a while. When she got in, her phone started beeping almost immediately. Messages coming in, one after the other.

She pulled her phone out of the evening bag. From Drew.

miss you already

can't wait for dinner tonight

wasn't ready for the night to be over

It was a painful inward struggle to keep herself from telling the driver to turn right around and take her back. She could not make a fool of herself and get all goofy about him. Just. Could. Not.

She tapped in same but then the emoji menu beckoned. Should she add a smiley face, a kissy face, heart eyes, a throbbing heart? Fruits and vegetables? Damn.

Keep it restrained, she reminded herself. Dignified. Not goofy.

She finally went with it was a wonderful night. No emojis.

my pillows smell like your perfume he responded.

Oh, God, he was killing her. She scrolled down the emoticon menu again. Picked out a single flower emoji, and sent it. Restraint. Restraint was everything.

Then she sat there, face red, heart thudding. Toes curling in her shoes. Waiting like a lovesick ninny for his response. It didn't take long.

aloof and mysterious as always

The driver gave her a doubtful look in the rearview as she laughed out loud.

hardly she replied, and then added three flame emojis and a lipstick kiss.

After a moment, going for a run to burn off excess energy. text you after.

She wished she could see Drew Maddox running. That big, sleek, stunning body in motion, bounding along, radiating heat, all flushed and sweatily gorgeous.

Mmm. Yes, please.

sounds good. enjoy yourself she tapped in.

Excess energy, ha. They'd made love five times, counting the shower time, and slept hardly at all. But she was buzzing with plenty of excess energy herself. She was restless and fidgety, and wanted to break into a song-and-dance routine on the street. But she contained herself, with some effort.

When she got to her apartment, she was relieved not to see her landlady or any of her neighbors. Smudge made his displeasure with her known the moment she walked in. She hastened to feed him and placate him, but he was having none of it, ignoring her frostily as he wolfed down his breakfast.

She plugged her phone in to charge and headed to the bedroom, picking out a burgundy wool dress suit with a short sixties-style skirt that made her feel like Audrey Hepburn. After a shower, she tried twisting her hair up into a tidy bun, but as usual, ended up looking like a burning bush. Sleek was just never going to be her thing.

As soon as she got her makeup on, she heard the rapid-fire beeping of text alerts. She lunged for the phone. It could be Drew.

It wasn't. Two missed calls from Ava, and a whole bunch of messages.

?? where are you?

didn't we have a coffee date at Ruby's to run over the Bricker Foundation stuff?

c'mon Jenna, I have things to tell you and a busy as hell day!

Oh, cripes. She'd asked Ava to give her feedback on the spiel she was going to give Bev's friends from the Bricker Foundation. All the drama had wiped that appointment completely out of her mind.

She tapped in a quick response.

sorry, running late. On my way. Hang tight.

A frowning emoji arrived and then, I'll order for you. cinnamon buns good today.

She gave Smudge an apologetic belly rub and got her thumb bitten, less gently than usual. Message received. She grabbed her car keys.

She got lucky with parking, and trotted into Ruby's panting and red-faced. Ava sat in her usual booth with her laptop out and a pair of severe black reading glasses perched on her nose that somehow only managed to accentuate how ridiculously pretty she was. Her honey-blond hair was loose and swirling down over her black sweater. She looked up at Jenna, and her eyebrow climbed.

She lifted a cup. "Vanilla latte, triple shot," she said. "Because I am a good friend."

"Thanks." Jenna slid into the booth and took a grateful sip of the hot beverage.

"So before we take a quick look at the Bricker Foundation stuff for today, let me just show you these stats," she started briskly. "Ernest and I were talking about the big picture for Arm's Reach last night, and it's fantastic, the progress we've made."

"Um, about that," Jenna said. "I appreciate everything you've done, Av, but I need to back off for a little while."

"Back off?" Ava looked horrified. "That's insane. Your visibility is through the roof. You show up first on every search. You're trending everywhere. You've been telling a juicy story, and everyone's paying attention to it. You can't stop now!"

"But that's just the thing, Av. You're a storyteller. I'm not. I'm a scientist. I like facts. Hard data. Not stories."

"Sure, but this is all in the service of science, Jenn.

Oh, hey. Speaking of facts and hard data, where in the hell were you this morning?"

Jenna choked on her coffee and sputtered into a napkin. "Excuse me?"

"I went to your apartment, since I was up early," Ava said. "You weren't there, but your car was, so I knew you hadn't gone to work. So what gives?"

Jenna almost blurted out the truth, but something stopped her. And she couldn't even lie and say she'd gone jogging, or to an early spin class. Her face got hotter. She couldn't meet Ava's eyes.

Ava took a bite of cinnamon bun, frowning in puzzlement. Then she stopped chewing, and just stared at Jenna's face, her eyes going wide.

"No way." Her voice was flat. "You didn't."

Jenna pressed her hands against her hot cheeks. She didn't bother to deny it. It seemed ridiculous to lie, after last night's huge, public scene. She tried to laugh it off. "It's so surprising to you? After what you saw last night?"

Ava swallowed her bite of pastry with evident difficulty. "I thought you were just, ah…you know. That it was all part of the, um…"

"Story? Good Lord, Ava, do you think I'd roll around half-dressed in front of the Board of Directors and your uncle just for a boost in my search engine optimization? How slutty and cynical do you think I am?"

"Not at all." Ava's voice was tight and colorless. "So you and Drew are…a thing now?"

Her friend sounded both incredulous and worried. Both reactions bugged the hell out of her. "It's so improbable to you?"

Ava didn't bother responding to that. "Since when has this been going on?"

"We've been circling around it since the very beginning," Jenna admitted. "But last night is the first time that we, uh…"

"Did the deed," Ava finished.

An appalled silence spread between them. The concerned look in Ava's eyes was driving Jenna nuts. "Don't look like that! Cripes, is it such a terrible development?"

Ava shook her head. "That's not it. I think you're wonderful. You know that. I just…it's just…" Ava's voice trailed off. She was uncharacteristically lost for words.

Icy clarity settled in, along with an ache of dread that threatened to completely dampen her buzz of excitement.

"You don't think I can hold his interest," she said flatly. "You don't think I can measure up to all his movie stars and models."

Ava dismissed the movie stars and models with a flap of her hand. "Not at all," she said impatiently. "They were a bunch of airheads, mostly. He was with them because they were cute and right there in front of him, so why not. Besides, he never wants to risk actually caring about somebody with substance, so I never thought that he would actually…"

"So you don't think we're believable as a couple," Jenna said. "Believable for the Maddox Hill Board of Directors, and your uncle, maybe, because playacting is fine. But not for real."

"Don't be mad," Ava pleaded. "When I proposed this to him, I never in a million years thought that—"

"That he could actually be interested in someone like me," Jenna finished.

"Don't put words in my mouth," Ava snapped. "It never occurred to me that this could have, you know, consequences. That I could set you up for disappointment, or hurt. You've had enough already. I didn't think it through, that's all. And that…scares me."

Well, great. That made two of them.

Jenna got up and grabbed her coffee. "Thanks for the vote of confidence. If you'll excuse me, I have a busy day ahead, so have a good one."

"Don't forget that tomorrow morning, you and Drew have that interview with the—"

"No," Jenna broke in. "Cancel the interview. Cancel everything. Say I'm sick. Say anything you want. I can't handle any more PR events. I'm done playacting, I'm sick of being photographed. I appreciate your hard work and I think you're a genius, but the price is too high. As of today, Project Billionaire's Plaything is on indefinite hiatus."

"Jenn. Please." The tone in Ava's voice stopped her in her tracks. Her friend never sounded like that. Dead serious. Subdued.

"What?" she snapped.

"Just please. Be careful," Ava said.

That made her even more miserable. She'd spent weeks convinced that Drew could never be interested in her for real, and now look at her—all bent out of shape because Ava thought the exact same thing.

It was hypocritical and unfair.

She hurried toward her car. The text alert chirped as she got in. Then another. Two messages from Drew, responding to a picture she'd sent him of Smudge, glaring up at her over his chicken chunks.

Your cat fits my color scheme. He would look good in my living room.

Or I maybe I should say, my living room would look good on your cat.

Oh, man. Tears welled into her eyes.

All the feels. Floodgates open. His offhand remark unleashed wild fantasies of domestic bliss with Drew. Feeding chicken chunks to her kitty in his kitchen. Smudge curled up on his couch.

When he said things like that, how the hell was she supposed to stay careful?

Eighteen

The meeting about engineering problems in the Abu Dhabi project ran an extra hour over, but Drew was in too good a mood to be upset. Maybe he wasn't going to have to resign from his position after all. Which was a huge relief. Fingers crossed. For all of it, including Jenna.

He was on cloud nine after that night with her. He never allowed himself to look at his phone in meetings, but he could feel the phone vibrate in his pocket whenever she sent him a message. The constant buzz of anticipation kept his spirits sky-high, even with Harold giving him the fish-eye.

Eventually he was going to have to do something about his cousin's poisonous hostility, but today he couldn't be bothered to worry about it. He had better things to think about. Like Jenna's texts.

He usually felt annoyed and oppressed when his

lovers texted him during a workday. He liked keeping things compartmentalized. Work was work, and he liked a hard focus.

Not an option with Jenna. She was interconnected with every thought in his head.

As they came out of the meeting, he already had his phone in his hand but was still talking to his VPs, including Harold. "Make sure you talk to Michaela and Loris about those budget details before you move forward," Drew said.

"Of course," his cousin drawled. "Look at you. In such a good mood today."

Drew gave him a wary look. "Why shouldn't I be?"

"I just expected you to look more hungover, considering the condition you were in last night," Harold said.

"I didn't drink last night," he said.

Harold snorted. "If you say so. Must be the health benefits of rolling around in bed with Jenna Somers. Guess I can't really blame you. She is red-hot."

Drew waited for a couple of breaths before he replied. "Don't say her name again," he said. "Don't even get near her. Or we will have a problem."

"Oh, yeah? You going to go all tough ex-Marine on me and rearrange my face?"

"If that's the only thing you understand," Drew replied. "Bring it."

"Break it up, boys." Ava's crisp voice came from behind them. "Harry, whatever your damn problem is, put it on ice and excuse us, please. I urgently need to speak to Drew. Alone."

Harold made a disgusted sound and stalked away.

Drew turned toward his sister. "Thanks for shutting him up. Uncle Malcolm wouldn't appreciate me breaking his jaw during working hours."

"Don't thank me yet," Ava said icily. "You're not going to be grateful when I'm done with you."

Tension gripped him. "Why? What have I done now?"

"Let's talk in your office, please."

Drew knew what this was about. He strode toward his office, Ava keeping pace beside him, and held the door for her. When the door closed behind them, he braced himself and turned. "Okay. Let me have it."

"What in holy hell do you think you're doing?" Ava burst out.

He sighed. "Help me out here, Av. Context, please."

"Don't you dare play dumb!" Ava said furiously. "I never meant for you to seduce her! That is self-indulgent and irresponsible!"

Drew let out a harsh laugh. "You threw her into my arms yourself."

"Is that what you think I did? That I just gave you license to amuse yourself?"

"Amuse myself?" Drew bristled. "What the hell, Av? She's a grown woman!"

"She's not like your usual type. You know. All the Lydia clones."

"Lydia is not my type," he snarled.

"Well, if Lydia herself was ever confused about that, I wouldn't blame her," Ava said. "I thought you understood. This was a little bit of theater to help you over a bad spot, and goose the stats for Jenna's company, and now you decide to have a taste? Of my best friend? What the hell were you thinking?"

Drew spoke through his teeth. "You're pissing me off."

"Yeah? Well, the feeling is mutual." Ava's voice was low and furious. "I love Jenna. And I mean, for real love her, get me? She's the kindest, most selfless, principled person I know. She is not a disposable squeeze toy for you to play around with!"

"What makes you think I'm playing?"

His sister laughed harshly. "Oh, I don't know." Her voice was heavy with irony. "Your track record? You bore easily, big brother. Don't think I or the rest of the world hasn't noticed. You've left a trail of high-profile, royally pissed-off women in your wake. If you do that to my girl Jenna, I will rip your head right off your neck."

"It's not that I bore easily," Drew said. "I've just been choosing badly."

"Seriously?" Ava shook her head in disbelief. "You just now realized, at the ripe old age of thirty-four, that you should maybe take something other than a pretty face and a hot body into consideration when choosing a lover? Wow, Drew! Boom! Blinding insight, huh? Congratulations! Better late than never, I guess!"

He turned his back on her and stared out at the view. "I don't get this," he said. "If you think she's so fabulous, what made you think I wouldn't notice?"

Ava made a frustrated sound. "I don't know. I just didn't think it through. I never would have imagined the two of you together, because you…" Her voice trailed off.

Drew stared her down. "You think I'm not good enough for her," he said.

Ava bit her lip. Her angry flush had faded. "No. I didn't say that."

But she'd hesitated too long for her denial to be convincing.

They were locked in an awful silence, unable to look away from each other.

Finally Ava shook it off. "Damn it, Drew. Just don't lead her on, okay? I don't want to be responsible for that. It would suck if she got hurt and it was all my fault."

He walked over to the door. "Get out." He opened it for her.

The crowd of people gathered outside suddenly turned away and wandered off with extreme nonchalance. Damn. So they'd been yelling loud enough to be heard through the expensively sealed soundproofed door. Ava stalked out, chin high, lips tight.

Drew closed the door after her, leaning against it. Stung.

He wondered if Jenna felt like Ava did. That he was faithless and irresponsible. Good for nothing but sex. A dog on the furniture, like his uncle said. He wondered if she was just amusing herself while keeping her shields up and her heart fully armored.

It didn't feel like that was the case, but it would serve him right if it was.

Ava and all the rest of them could all go to hell. He'd make this work. He could be a better man for her. He'd show her. If it took years. A lifetime.

This was the first time that the concept of spending a lifetime with one woman made sense to him.

Roddy's song ran through his head, along with a powerful sense memory of that soul-melding kiss they'd shared at the Wild Side. Roddy had nailed it with those lyrics.

He'd found his reason why. He was all hers. It was a done deal. On his part, at least.

All that was left was to convince her that he was for real.

"So, Jenna. Enough business. Let's dish a little. We're all so excited about your upcoming wedding!" Helen Sanderson said. "Give us some juicy details!"

Jenna looked around the table at the older ladies, all

Bev's philanthropist friends from the Bricker Foundation, who were smiling at her expectantly.

"Um, we don't actually have firm plans yet," she hedged.

"Well, we certainly can help with that," Jayne Braithwaite said eagerly. "We have experience in these kinds of things. All of us have helped our kids get married."

"It was such a shock to hear that Drew Maddox finally got lassoed," Margot Kristoff confided. "That boy always was way too handsome. It's so satisfying when one of those types finally figures out what's good for him."

"Hendrick was like that, years ago," Bev mused with a nostalgic air.

The other ladies all chuckled. "He figured out what side his bread was buttered on quick enough," Helen said.

"Exactly," Bev said. "And that's what I hope for you, honey."

Jenna forced herself to smile. "Me, too."

"Did you ever see Drew in his dress uniform?" Gwen Hoyt asked, miming fanning herself. "Oh me, oh my."

"Only pictures, I'm afraid," she said. "I wish. I'm sure he looks stunning."

"My husband was in the air force, see," Gwen confided. "And that uniform just did something to me. I just love to see a man in a dress uniform."

"So, sweetie," Jayne said briskly. "The Wexler Prize Awards Banquet is coming up in just a few weeks. Are you shopping for the ultimate dress and writing your acceptance speech?"

"Oh, it's by no means a sure thing," Jenna said.

"There are many excellent candidates. They're all fabulous projects."

"True, but I put my money on you," Bev said. "In any case, everyone wants to put money on you right now. The Maddox Hill Foundation is interested in partnering with Arm's Reach, and so is the Bricker Foundation. There's so much buzz about you! Seems like you can't turn around without seeing another photo of you and Drew, or hearing something about Arm's Reach. You're on everyone's lips!"

Jenna felt freshly guilty for being so angry with Ava at the coffee shop. "That's completely Ava's doing," she said. "She's a marketing genius."

"That she is," Bev agreed. "That girl is a live wire. But the magic was there to begin with, honey. She just shone a brighter light on it so everyone could see."

"Thank you." Jenna's face went hot.

Helen reached out and grabbed her hand. "So, you haven't set a date yet?"

"Not really," Jenna said. "We've just been kicking ideas around."

"If you're getting married close to home, your best bet is May through September," Gayle advised. "But always with an indoor option."

"My brother-in-law runs a gorgeous resort on the coast," Margot told her. "It's called Paradise Point. It's on this spit of land that juts out on the coast. Sea cliffs, beaches below, fields of wildflowers, crashing waves, stunning views. There's even a lighthouse and rock monoliths on the beach. And the resort itself is a gem. Drew designed the building, you know."

"No, I, uh, didn't know that."

"Here, look at this." Margot leaned over the table,

showing Jenna her phone. "These are some of the pictures I took of my niece Brooke's wedding at Paradise Point last year. Enchanting place. And would you believe, it drizzled the whole time, but because of the way the building was designed, we never felt like we were trapped indoors. That's what I love about Drew's designs."

"Agreed," Jenna said. "His house is like that, too. It feels so soothing."

The older ladies exchanged delighted glances that she pretended not to see as she swiped through Margot's photos. "Isn't that just sweet?" Bev murmured. "He talks that way about her work, too. They're so proud of each other. I just love that."

"So next summer, then?" Jayne prompted. "Or did you want spring flowers?"

"Oh, good, I finally found it," Margot said, holding up her phone again. "This is my favorite. This is Brooke and her new husband, Matthias, the moment that the rain stopped and the sun came through. Look, how the photographer actually caught them framed in a rainbow. Isn't that just precious?"

Jenna looked at the picture. A pretty blonde held up the muddied hem of her wedding dress, gazing adoringly up into the face of a stocky, beaming young black-haired man. All around them, sunlight had broken through the clouds, highlighting the flowers.

And a rainbow arched over them. It was unbearably perfect. The couple looked so happy.

The feelings came over her too fast to fend off. She dove for a tissue. Margot pushed one into her hand before she found them. The older women clustered around murmuring in consternation.

Bev grabbed her hand. "Sweetie, are you okay?"

"I'm fine," she said. "These photos are so beautiful, and I'm just so damn emotional right now. Everything sets me off."

Bev pressed her hand. "You sure you're fine?"

Jenna dabbed carefully under her eyes. "I'm great. It's just that it's too new to talk about wedding venues. Seeing the pictures of Brooke and her husband—it's just too much. I'm so happy right now, but I'm still afraid of jinxing myself. Sorry."

"Don't apologize," Margot said gently. "That picture makes me cry, too, and I've been married for forty-two years. We're all just so happy for you. Sorry we pushed you, honey."

"We all know how risky it is," Bev said. "Loving someone, marrying him. You just have to cross your fingers and hope to God you don't crash and burn."

Jayne squeezed her shoulder. "We're rooting for you. You seem like a lovely girl."

Jenna looked around at their kindly faces, and her eyes got misty again. She wanted so badly for this relationship to be real, and worthy of all this benevolent well-wishing. But she wasn't even convinced herself yet. It was premature, to talk about wedding venues.

Too much, too soon. It was a recipe for disaster.

Nineteen

"Drew, will you do up these hooks for me?"

Drew finished buttoning his tux shirt and came up behind Jenna, who stood in front of the big standing mirror he'd gotten a couple of weeks ago for his bedroom. He'd never felt the need for one before, but now he had Jenna in his space, dressing for work, putting on her makeup, doing her hair. A beautiful woman like her needed a full-length mirror to put herself together.

He paused for a moment to admire her. The low-cut, midnight blue taffeta evening dress consisted of a tight-fitting strapless boned bodice of textured taffeta that showcased her elegant curves and narrow waist, billowing out into a big, full, rustling skirt.

The bodice was open over her back, showing the long, graceful curve of her spine and the delicate shadow of her shoulder blades, her fine-grained, flawless skin. The enticing shadow of her cleavage. Lust stabbed into him, predictably enough.

Jenna shot him a glance as he placed his hands on her waist and slid them up until he was cupping her breasts. "So fine." His voice was a sexy rasp.

She fluttered her lashes at him seductively. "Be that as it may, we can't be late. Don't be bad."

Her voice had that breathless catch that it got when he succeeded in tempting her.

"They'll wait for us." He bent down to press a hot kiss against the back of her neck, making a delicious shiver of sensual awareness vibrate through her body.

"Oh, no you don't," she murmured. "Don't make me all sweaty and damp and have to fix my makeup all over again."

"I'll make it worth your while," he coaxed.

"Save it," she said sternly. "You'll get what you want…but later."

He bowed to the inevitable, but took his own sweet time with the tiny hooks, relishing the opportunity to touch her hot, petal-smooth skin as he fastened them up. Admiring all the details. The shape of her spine, her elegant posture, the shape of her shoulder blades.

He'd liked the way his life felt, these last weeks. Liked it so much, it scared him.

Ava had eased off on the punishing PR schedule, thank God, so he and Jenna had been able to spend some free time together. He was greedy for all of it, so bit by bit, she'd started spending most of the time at his house—along with her cat.

Smudge wasn't quite sure about Drew yet. He kept trying to establish dominance. But even that couldn't put a damper on how much Drew loved having Jenna in his living space.

"One moment, for the full effect," she murmured, adjusting the cups of the bodice. Afterwards, her perfect high breasts spilled out of the top of the cups just enough to make Drew slightly uncomfortable.

"I could have adjusted that for you, too," he told her.

"And then we would have ended up being late. I know you." Her mouth was stern, but her eyes smiled.

"You look fantastic," he told her.

It was the stark truth. He couldn't stop staring. The deep blue made her skin glow like it was lit from inside. The design hugged her stunning figure. Her blue satin spike-heeled shoes had delicate, glittering ankle straps. He ached to touch her.

"Which glasses today?" he asked. "The blue ones?"

"Contacts, for special occasions. The announcement of the Wexler Prize is a special occasion. I'm not wearing workaday specs for that."

"You know that your specs make me hot," he told her.

"No, Drew, you just exist in a generally overheated state, and the specs are incidental. Not that I'm complaining. I like having you perpetually ready for action."

"Always," he promised. "The dress looks great on you."

"It ought to, considering what it cost," she said, fastening her little diamond drop earrings into her ears with a secret smile. "I still think it was extravagant of you. My other dress would have been fine."

"I wanted you to get this dress because it looks good with this other thing I got you," he told her.

Her eyes filled with alarm. "Drew. We talked about this. Remember?"

"Yes, yes. I know. No billionaire's-plaything scenarios. Not even as fun, lighthearted bed-play. We're just two people enjoying each other's company. No mind games. No power plays. No expensive gifts. All of this is forbidden. Rules are rules."

"Good," she said cautiously. "Then… What did you do?"

"This." He pulled a teardrop sapphire pendant, ringed with smaller diamonds, out of his pocket and held it up in front of her. It settled right at the hollow of her throat as he fastened the clasp of the delicate, glittering white gold chain.

Jenna gasped. "Oh, my God, Drew. I can't accept this."

"I found it a couple weeks ago. I thought it would look perfect with the ring. That was why I pushed for blue, even though the other dresses looked great on you, too."

"But… It's against the rules." Her hand went up to touch it delicately.

"Sometimes rules have to be broken. That nugget of wisdom brought to you by Michael Wu, who has finally kicked my underperforming ass up to level eight. He advised me to be bolder and risk harder, or else I'll just keep running around in the same circles."

She gazed at herself in the mirror, wide-eyed. "Very smooth," he said. "Video game wisdom, to manipulate me. You know that Michael is my soft spot."

"I love manipulating your soft spots," he whispered into her ear. "I'll use whatever works. But Michael's logic makes sense to me. Because I think we're ready."

She turned to look up at him. "For what?"

"The next level," he said.

They just gazed at each other. The air hummed with emotion. Endless possibilities.

He took her hand, and kept kissing it until he felt that subtle shift of energy, like the wind ruffling the grass. They were so attuned to each other. God, how he loved that.

Her eyes dropped. "This isn't a conversation to have when we're late to an important function," she said. "Let's, um, hit Pause. Pick this up later."

He let out a sigh. At least it wasn't a flat-out no. But he wanted so badly to nail this down and close the deal. "You will wear the necklace, though, right?" he wheedled.

She narrowed her eyes at him, fingering the pendant. "You are sneaky."

"Always," he assured her.

"Hmmph. This time," she conceded. "I have to go find my evening bag. I think I left it in the studio."

The skirt swooshed and rustled past his legs as she swept out, leaving him alone and secretly exulting. It was a huge deal that she was wearing jewelry he'd gotten her. She was so prickly about the billionaire-plaything vibe. Every little silly detail made her twitchy.

He looked around for his tux jacket and found it on the bed, with Smudge curled up on top of it, purring loudly.

As Drew approached, Smudge rolled onto his back and stretched luxuriously, flopping this way and that, making sure to cover the entire jacket. Then he flipped over and began digging his claws into the shiny black lapels, kneading them. His golden eyes fixed on Drew's face, waiting to see how he took it.

Drew sighed. "I need my tux jacket, cat."

He picked the cat up and dropped him on the floor. Smudge hissed and stalked away with his tail high to plot his next move.

The jacket was hot, creased and crumpled and covered with a layer of downy gray fluff. Drew got the lint roller, an item that now hung on the closet door for easy and constant access, and rolled the cat fluff carefully off from his jacket.

This was next-level stuff for sure.

The first part of the evening passed in a daze for Jenna. She had to hope that her mind was functioning on autopilot during the mix-and-mingle part of the evening, because she'd talked with what felt like hundreds of people and had not the slightest memory of what she'd said to them. She just kept touching the pendant at her throat and trying to keep herself from dancing with excitement.

Next level? What exactly did that mean, other than the screamingly obvious? She didn't dare get it wrong. Could she have misunderstood, projected, overshot his intentions? She was head over heels in love, and he kept luring her deeper into his life.

And it was so much fun. She slept at his house every night. Weekend mornings were coffee and sex and brunch, then more sex. Evenings they cooked dinner together, cuddled on the couch or on his terrace on the lake, sipping a glass of brandy under a cashmere blanket, legs wound together on the hassock. He'd dedicated a studio for her so she could work weekends from his house. He'd installed a cat door in his kitchen for Smudge. He'd designated a huge closet for her, as if she had a wardrobe vast enough to fill it.

And then, relentlessly, he was filling it. Like this gown, for instance. It was stunning, but it was total billionaire-plaything nonsense, the very kind she'd forbidden from the very beginning. Now the sapphire pendant, for God's sake. To match the ring.

He was getting bolder.

She wondered if she'd be required to spend obscene amounts of his money on dressing herself at the next level. Hmm.

She'd cross that bridge when she came to it.

At some point in the evening, Bev and her friends and colleagues from the Bricker Foundation ganged up on her and towed her away from Drew to introduce her to someone, and she quickly got embroiled in a lively discussion about partnership possibilities with a charity that helped the victims of land mines. Afterward, she strolled through the ballroom, scanning for Drew. It seldom took long to find him, even in a big crowd, he was so tall. And no one filled out a tux like that man.

"Jenna," said a familiar voice from behind her.

She spun around with a gasp and beheld Rupert, all dressed up in a tuxedo.

"What in the hell are you doing here?" she demanded.

"Way to make a guy feel welcome." Rupert sounded a little hurt.

Like he had any right to expect a welcome from her. But she suppressed a tart reply. There were people all around and she was tired of being the floor show.

"What are you doing here, Rupert?" she asked again.

"I was invited," he said huffily. "You do remember that I worked on these projects, right? The Wexler Foundation sent the invitation to the whole team." He tossed back the rest of his champagne and smacked it down with far too much force on the tray of a passing server, causing all the champagne flutes on the tray to totter and sway. By some miracle of coordination, the server managed not to drop them all, but Rupert didn't even notice.

"I knew they sent an invitation to the team, but I didn't expect to see you come," Jenna said. "I thought you were in Bali. Where's Kayleigh? Didn't she come with you?"

Rupert's face tightened. "Ah. Well, no. About that. It's over with Kayleigh. I came back early from Bali."

"It's over? You mean…"

"Finished," Rupert said glumly. "We broke up."

Jenna realized that her mouth was hanging open, and closed it. "Oh. That was quick."

He shrugged. "Can I speak with you?"

"You're speaking with me now, aren't you?"

"I mean in private. Please."

Jenna glanced around at the murmuring crowd filling the ballroom of the stunning Crane Convention Center, one of Maddox Hill's newest projects. "Rupert, I'm really busy tonight, and this isn't the time or place."

"Please," he urged. "Just a word. It won't take long. You owe me that."

Actually, she didn't owe him a damn thing. But she didn't want to make a scene and she also wanted to be done with this, whatever it was. That way, she didn't have to schedule another encounter. Things were always better dealt with hot and on the spot.

She sighed silently, and gestured for him to follow her. She led the way out of the ballroom and swiftly up the sweeping double staircase, to the luxury suite that Maddox Hill reserved for its own use. In this case, it had served as a headquarters for the event planners. It was deserted now, since all the event coordinators were downstairs, on the job.

"Okay, Rupert," she said crisply. "Dinner's about to be served. After that, they're going to award the Wexler Prize, and I'm really hoping to win it. So please, make it snappy."

"I see you're as career oriented as you ever were," he commented.

That got her goat, but she didn't rise to the bait. "You better believe it," she agreed, noting his peeling sunburn from too much beach in Bali and his affected little goatee. And the smug, superior expression on his face. Thank God, she'd stopped short of marrying that. She was so grateful. "Tell me."

"I'm not sure just how to say this to you, Jenna—"

"Figure it out fast."

He looked hurt. "You're being sharp."

She gave him a look. "Do you blame me?"

His expression softened. "No," he said earnestly. "I truly do not. Jenna, I've learned so much about myself in the past few weeks. That's what I wanted to tell you."

She stifled a groan. Just what her evening lacked. To hear what Rupert had learned about himself. "It's not a good time," she repeated, through her teeth.

"It was a mistake," Rupert said. "Getting involved with Kayleigh, I mean. I got carried away. It was an illusion. All lust and hormones. I just didn't realize who she really was."

It took all her self-control not to roll her eyes. "Really? What tipped you off?"

She immediately regretted the question, because Rupert didn't get the irony. "She had an affair," he said, his voice cracking with emotion. "Just days after our wedding. With the yoga instructor. At the honeymoon resort."

Jenna managed somehow not to laugh and tell him that karma was a bitch. "That's awful," she said. "How disappointing."

"I knew you'd understand." Rupert's eyes were soulful. "I have no right to say this, after what happened, but you are just…radiant tonight. I've never seen you look so beautiful."

Compliments from Rupert made her uneasy. She shifted back a step. "Um. Thanks."

"It's so strange. Almost as if it took that stupid, squalid adventure with Kayleigh to actually be able to see you clearly, for what you are. The contrast between you and her, you know? It's like, I never saw you… And now I'm dazzled. A veil has been lifted."

Jenna was horrified. "Rupert, don't."

"Please, let me finish. You're the only one for me. I'm sorry it took me so long to figure that out. I'm so sorry I ever let you down."

Jenna backed away from him. "I don't know if you've been paying attention, but I'm involved with someone else right now," she said cautiously. "I mean, seriously involved."

"Yes, and that's another thing." Rupert's voice took on that maddening tone it got when he decided to school her about something. "I know you might be dazzled by Drew Maddox. He's rich and famous, and all that. But I've heard stories—"

"Hold it right there. I'm not interested in hearing sleazy gossip about my boyfriend, and from you, of all people. Just don't."

"He'll be unfaithful to you," Rupert informed her.

Amazing, that he could say it with a straight face. "Are you listening to yourself?"

"Of course I am," he said huffily.

She realized, with a flash of understanding, that had been the problem all along. He listened to himself only. That was the difference between him and Drew. One of the many. Drew actually heard what she said. Rupert never had.

"You cheated on me with Kayleigh, and you dare to preach to me?" she said.

"I learned from my mistakes," Rupert said loftily. "And I suffered for them. I doubt very much that Drew Maddox will. From what I read, he's not even capable of—"

"Shut up, Rupert," she said. "I don't want to hear about your mistakes, or your suffering. And don't say a word about Drew."

"I'm sorry to distress you, but you have to face the facts," Rupert said, in lofty tones. "Truth hurts, Jenna."

"So does a broken jaw."

Drew's voice sounded from behind them, low and soft with controlled rage.

Twenty

Jenna spun around, horrified. "Drew?"

Drew studied that son of a bitch looming over Jenna through a haze of red. His hands clenched. "What are you doing up here alone with this loser?"

"He wanted a word with me," Jenna said tartly. "And I didn't want to have an audience for this conversation. I'm tired of my life being public performance art."

Rupert shrank back as Drew strode over to stand behind Jenna, giving the man a stare that was calculated to make him squirm and sweat.

"Would you excuse us, Jenna?" he said. "I'd like to talk to this guy in private."

Rupert was now edging along the wall toward the door. *Good. Be afraid, jerkwad.*

"Why?" Jenna demanded. "You have nothing to say to him."

"I have plenty to say to a guy who's trying to move in on my fiancée." Drew kept his eyes fixed on the guy, tracking his every move. Rupert's forehead was getting shiny.

"The answer is no," Jenna said sharply. "I'm not going anywhere while you have that look on your face."

Rupert was almost at the door, still sliding along with his back to the wallpaper. "Come with me, Jenna!" he begged, holding out his hand to her as if to a drowning person. "We belong together! You deserve better than a…a degenerate playboy!"

Jenna sighed heavily. "Rupert, go. And I mean, right now. Leave the building."

"You had your chance, and you blew it." Drew's voice was low and menacing. "Stay the hell away from her. Or I will destroy you."

Rupert stumbled out the door and disappeared.

After a moment's stunned silence, Jenna turned to Drew, her eyes bright with outrage. "You'll destroy him? Did I really hear you say that?"

"I meant every word," Drew said. "That son of a bitch was making a move on you. Am I supposed to pretend I don't notice?"

"No!" she said sharply. "You're supposed to actually not notice! Rupert doesn't count! He's not your rival, he's just a silly, self-involved jerk. Nothing he says should be taken seriously!"

It took Drew a moment to work up the nerve to say it. "What about me?" he asked. "Do you take me seriously?"

Jenna looked startled at the question. She gazed at him for a moment.

"Yes," she said finally. "I do, absolutely. There is no comparison between you and him."

A sigh of relief came out of him. "So you don't still have feelings for him?"

She let out an incredulous laugh. "For Rupert? Oh, God, no. You were jealous?"

"Yes," he admitted. "I wanted to kill the guy."

"Oh, please. I never did have feelings for him, not really. I just convinced myself that I did, because I had nothing to compare it to."

"Meaning that now you do?"

Her face flushed. "Well, yes. As I'm sure you can guess."

"I could guess," he said. "But I don't want to. Not anymore. Spell it out for me."

Jenna let out a long, shaky breath. "I never felt for him what I feel for you."

He just kept on waiting. "So far, so good, but I'm still in suspense. What do you feel for me?"

She let out a shaky laugh. "Wow, you're relentless tonight."

"I just walked in here and found another man trying to steal my lady," Drew said. "I need some reassurance. So sue me."

"How's this for reassurance?" Jenna wound her arms around his neck and kissed him.

Reality shifted on its axis, like it always did when they touched. Desire flared up, hot and immediate. She wrapped her leg around his legs and braced herself, her breasts pressing against his tux shirt. Melting for him, straining to get closer. Locked in a breathless kiss.

Jenna lifted her head when she felt cool air on her

bare back. He'd undone some of the hooks of her dress. She pulled away, laughing and shaking her head. "Oh, no you don't! You're not getting my clothes off any place where people could burst in on us. Never again. I haven't even processed the trauma from the last time."

He looked around, and pulled her into the bathroom, flipping the door lock and switching on the light. Two soft-focus lights from wall sconces lit the flesh-toned marble of the bathroom. She was so beautiful, her eyes dazed, cheeks pink, red lips softly parted as he hoisted her up onto the wide sink, pushing up the big, rustling armfuls of midnight blue taffeta until he found her hot, smooth skin above the thigh-high stockings.

He slid his hands higher, to the tender, secret flesh. Stroking her with teasing fingertips, making her melt and writhe and press his hand against herself, demanding more.

He sank down to his knees, pushing taffeta out of his way and tugging her small blue satin thong panties down. He pressed his mouth to her tender secret folds.

Her hot, sweet taste was intoxicating. He could never get enough. The way she opened to him like a flower, and then melted into shivering pleasure, coming for him. A long, strong, lingering climax that made him feel like a god.

He held her there for a few minutes until the aftershocks gave way to the shimmering glow, and that was as much as he could stand. He needed her...right...now.

He rose up, unfastening his pants, and scooped up her legs, draping them over his arms. Her hands clutched at his shoulders, fingernails digging in as he eased himself slowly, insistently inside her.

She was exquisitely ready. She took him so deep. Every liquid, sliding stroke was unbearably perfect. She'd forgotten the rest of the world existed, and he was glad, because he loved those breathless whimpering sounds she made, until that deep, sensual pulsing rhythm of his thrusts made them shake apart.

He pulled slowly, reluctantly out of her, leaning his damp forehead against hers. Awestruck, like always.

He set her gently on the floor before he tucked his shirt back into his pants.

"Staking your claim much?" she asked shakily. But there was breathless laughter in her voice.

Drew took his time in responding, washing his face in the sink. "If that's what I was doing, expect me to keep doing it. I'll stake my claim every chance I get."

His phone buzzed in his pocket. A text from Zack.

Someone threw a rock through a window in the Azalea Room while they were setting up the dessert buffet. They're moving the buffet to the Rose Room.

"There's a situation downstairs," he said. "I need to check it out."

"I'll take a minute to put myself together," Jenna said. "See you back in the ballroom?"

"Yeah." He gave her a long, possessive kiss, then stepped back to watch as she smoothed and shook down her skirt. She started fixing her makeup. She was so damn gorgeous. It blew his mind.

Jenna slanted him an amused look. "Didn't you have someplace to be?"

Damn. "Yeah, guess so." He forced himself to back out. Closed the door after himself.

Kissing her had knocked Zack's message right out of his mind.

Being in love made it hard to concentrate.

Twenty-One

Jenna remained in the private suite for at least ten minutes before she could stand without wobbling. She washed up, freshened her makeup, adjusted her hair. She'd put her whole heart on the table for him. It made her giddy and scared.

She was as decent as she could make herself by the time she ventured out of that room, but her hot pink flush just wouldn't fade.

It would be all too easy to guess what she and Drew had been up to. All they had to do was look at her eyes, her cheeks, her hair. She was so sick of having her private life be everybody's entertainment.

"Jenna! I thought I might find you here."

She spun around with a squeak of alarm as a hand clamped her wrist. "Harold? What on earth—you scared me!"

"Just wanted a word." His eyes raked her up and down.

"Yeah, you and everyone else. Not now." She tugged at her wrist.

He didn't let go. "I just need a minute of your time. Could we slip into the suite to have a private—"

"Absolutely not," she said forcefully.

Harold shrugged. "Fine, but I have something to tell you and it's in your best interests to hear it behind closed doors. Trust me on this."

Trust him? *Ha.* "Right here is just fine," she said. "Make it quick."

Harold's eyes lingered on her flushed face, the smudges of makeup below her eyes, her cleavage. "I saw Drew strutting down the stairs like the cock of the walk," he said. "I can imagine what the two of you were up to in there. Fun, huh?"

"Get lost, Harold." She yanked again.

Harold held on, his fingers digging into her skin. "I'm trying to do you a favor."

"I'm doing just fine without any favors from you."

"Believe me, you'll be grateful." He held up his phone. "Have you seen this?"

Her eyes went to the screen, in spite of herself—and stiffened at what she saw.

The screen showed a photo of Drew, stretched out naked in a huge bed, apparently sleeping, and surrounded by naked women. And there was more—much more. Many women. The pictures flashed by, one after the other.

In all of them, Drew appeared to be unconscious.

Harold just watched her face avidly as she stared down at his screen. "Where did you get these photos?" she asked. "Who gave them to you?"

"Just what did Drew tell you about Sobel's party?" Harold asked.

"None of your business, Harold," she said.

"I know what he told my uncle," Harold said. "They knocked him down onto that couch and took compromising photos of him. Right? And that was all. He didn't tell you that he slunk out of that place the next morning after rolling around all night with a bunch of call girls. There's timed security footage of him walking out of that place at ten thirty-five. Word is, there are videos of the fun and games that happened during the night, too. Imagine how you'll feel when those videos drop."

She tried not to imagine it. There was a painful rock in her throat. "We are not having this conversation," she said. "Get the hell away from me."

"He's a liar, Jenna. Don't fall for it. You're smarter than that."

Jenna seized Harold's fingers, still clamped around her wrist, and pried them loose. She stepped back, rubbing her sore arm. There was a cold, sick weight in her belly. "I don't believe you," she said.

Harold's expression didn't change. "Those pictures don't care what you believe. Neither will anyone else who sees them. And they will see. They're viral already."

"All I saw was an unconscious man with some woman draped over him in bed," she said. "He told me he was ambushed. This doesn't disprove that."

Harold shook his head. "You are so far gone," he said, in a pitying tone. "What's it going to take to disillusion you?"

"A lot more than you've got," she told him.

Harold shrugged. "Your blind faith is touching but

pathetic. Let Drew sort out his own garbage. You have a career and reputation to protect. The more distance you get from him, the better off you'll be. Believe me. I'm trying to help."

"No, you're not," she said. "I've had people help me before. It doesn't feel like this."

Harold walked away, and Jenna stood like she'd been turned to stone. Her euphoria had been transformed into a gut-churning cold sweat. If those pictures really were doing the rounds on the internet, then things were going to get ugly for Drew in a big, public way. Tonight. She had to warn him.

At the same time, she was furious at him. Had he been making a fool of her, telling her it had just been photos that evening at Sobel's party? He'd said nothing to her about staying the night in a bed full of naked women and leaving the next morning.

Not that it was any of her business. It all happened before she'd gotten involved with him at all, to be absolutely fair. Still, if they'd videotaped him in that state, his goose was cooked. At least at Maddox Hill.

Was that what she had to look forward to? Her lover's sex tapes, doled out online one by one, with lots of buzz and buildup to a gleeful, greedy viewing public? It would be so awful.

She stopped next to the window overlooking the garden, pressing her forehead against the cold glass. God, what was it about her and men? Was she destined for this? Did she have a sign on her back? Gullible Nitwit. Please Lie to Me.

In any case, she didn't want him taken by surprise. She texted him. where r u?

She hurried down the stairs and caught sight of Vann,

Drew's CFO, muttering into a phone. He closed the call when he saw her.

"Vann, have you seen Drew?" she asked.

"Last I saw, he was heading over to the security station with Zack."

"Thanks." She stared down at her phone. Still nothing from Drew. She texted ?? and started trotting in that direction, tottering on those ridiculous heels. Then she stopped, and with a muttered obscenity, plucked the shoes off. She gathered up big armfuls of that huge skirt and ran in her stocking feet.

Zack gave her an odd look when she skidded into the security center sideways, pink and out of breath. "Jenna? What's up? Everything okay?"

"Fine," she said, panting. "But I need to find Drew. He's not answering my texts."

"I saw him heading back toward the ballroom a few minutes ago," Zack told her. He gestured toward the bank of security monitors. "Check those out. You might see him."

Jenna leaned over, peering at the images on various screens, one after the other. Drew didn't show up in any of them. Damn.

She turned to hurry out, but something on the last screen caught her eye. She turned back, leaning closer. That camera showed part of the grounds and the parking lot, and a tall man walking toward...*wait*.

Was that Harold? What...?

A car pulled up, and a woman was getting out of the back seat. She was tall and slim with a big cloud of curly blond hair. In the orange-tinted gloom of the parking lot, her eyes were smudgy pools of shadow. Harold took her arm, and she stumbled back against the car.

Harold pulled the tottering woman sharply after him and out of the camera's range. They looked like they were heading toward the side lobby, which was currently not in use.

Harold was up to something. She had to find out what it was. She didn't need any more damn surprises tonight, thank you very much.

Jenna ignored the security staff's puzzled looks as she took off once again, shoes swinging by their straps as she ran to the side lobby. No time to explain anything to anyone.

The eastern lobby was deserted. It had a large number of large, bushy plants in the vaulted atrium around a decorative waterfall that wasn't in use yet.

The big revolving door was shut, but someone had propped open the door beside it. Jenna slunk back against the wall behind the bushiest foliage as Harold and the woman with him appeared through the glass door.

They burst through it, arguing. Jenna slid back along the wall and into the recessed entry to the women's bathroom, gathering her skirt into a tight bundle to keep it quiet.

"You had one job, Tina. One. I said not to be late. Timing is everything tonight."

"I told you! I had a problem with Lauretta's bonehead boyfriend, and he—"

"I don't want to hear about it," Harold snarled. "Hurry!"

"I gotta stop at the bathroom," Tina said, her voice sulky. "When you're pregnant, you gotta pee all the time. I came all the way from Lauretta's house and it's, like, an hour and a half from here. So I—"

"We don't have time!" Harold urged.

Jenna's heart thudded as she slunk backward through the bathroom door, hoping it wouldn't creak. She dived into one of the stalls, locking it and climbing up onto the toilet, her skirt wound into a ball in her lap. Her phone chirped with an incoming message. Oh, no, no, no... Drew was finally responding to her texts. Freaking spectacular timing.

Jenna jerked the phone out of her evening bag with trembling hands, silenced it, then clicked open the audio recording app. She crouched there, balanced on her toes. Afraid to move or breathe as she heard Tina's shoes clicking against the bathroom floor.

Harold followed her in, still scolding. "Hurry up! We're missing it!"

Tina banged open the door of one of the stalls. "Why do you have to be so mean?"

"Why do you have to be so dumb?" Harold shot back. "And speaking of dumb, did you check the bathroom stalls?"

"No," Tina said, her voice sulky.

Jenna's teeth clenched as Harold swept the line of stalls, peering under the doors for feet. He didn't try to open any of the doors, to her intense relief.

"I don't deserve to be treated like crap," Tina said.

"I paid you." Harold's voice was icy cold. "We had an agreement."

"Yeah, well we also have a baby," Tina said, sniffling.

Harold made an impatient sound. "You signed the documents. You took the money. Do what I ask and don't give me trouble. Have the baby or don't, whatever you want, just don't involve me. He'll give you more money not to bust his balls, or else my uncle will. So shut up and be grateful."

"Why do I always get sucked into your schemes?" Tina complained. The toilet flushed loudly. "It's gross," she went on, when the noise abated. "Having me spray ketamine in your cousin's face was a real psycho move, Harry, and it was a monster dose, too. Poor guy was sick as a dog. You coulda killed him. And now I gotta go in front of all those people and tell them he got me pregnant? Why do you hate this dude so much? Did he, like, kill your puppy?"

"Hurry up, Tina. It's too late for a crisis of conscience."

She banged the stall door open again. Her heels clicked on her way to the sink. "I don't see why you even have to be this big-shot CEO at all." The water hissed as she washed her hands. "You're doin' fine. I've seen your house, your car. You got money. More'n I ever had, that's for sure. Can't we just be happy? With the baby?"

"You really think that scenario could ever make me happy, Tina? Wake up."

Tina turned the water off, sniffling loudly.

"Oh, for God's sake, don't start crying," Harold said impatiently. "We don't have time for this. Put your lipstick on. Come on, hurry!"

The door sighed closed after them, and clicked shut. Their squabbling voices faded away.

Jenna finally dared to exhale, teetering. She caught herself on the side of the bathroom stall, stepped down onto the bathroom floor. Her legs felt like jelly.

She ran the recording back, with ice-cold, clammy fingers, and clicked Play.

...we're missing it.

Why do you have to be so mean?

Why do you have to be so dumb? And speaking of dumb, did you check the bathroom stalls?

The voices were faint, but clear, and turning the volume up made Harold's nasal, drawling voice perfectly recognizable. Thank God.

She'd gotten it all, from the very beginning. But it wasn't going to do Drew a damn bit of good unless everyone heard it all at once, at the right moment, and before Harold's big fabricated bombshell.

Jenna edged out of the women's room and looked up the hall. Tina and Harold were just turning the corner, still snarking at each other as he dragged her along toward the ballroom. She couldn't go that way without overtaking them, and she wanted to get there first, without them knowing that she'd copped to their game.

The fastest alternative way back to the ballroom was outside, along the walkway skirting the building and back through the front entrance.

Jenna hurried out, barely feeling the frigid wind or the wooden planks beneath her feet as she ran. She hiked her skirt up and held her shoes with the other hand. They bounced against her leg with each step.

She stopped outside the lobby and stepped back into her shoes. A swift peek at her own reflection in the glass made her realize that at this point, there was just no way to salvage the up-do. Her hair needed to come down, once and for all. She plucked out the pins and shook her mane loose over her shoulders, finger-combing it as she hurried inside. She was flushed and her chest was heaving, but she was presentable.

She pushed through the double doors into the

dimmed ballroom. All lights were trained on the dais where the master of ceremonies stood, about to award the Wexler Prize.

Vann stepped out of the shadows, looking alarmed. "Jenna? What's going on? They're announcing the prize! Get over there with your team, quick!"

Jenna grabbed his arm. "Vann, I need your help. Can you run an audio recording that's on my phone onto the sound system of this room, right now? It's for Drew. To save his bacon. Please, please, please help me. Time is of the essence."

Vann's eyes widened. "Yes," he said swiftly. "Of course. Where is it?"

She pulled up the file and handed him her phone. "Listen for my cue," she said. "It was recorded in a bathroom stall, so crank up the volume to the max."

"...and this year's Wexler Prize for Excellence in Biomedical Engineering is awarded to...the Arm's Reach Foundation!"

The room erupted in thunderous applause.

"Go!" Vann whispered into her ear. "I got this."

Her team, gathered at the table that had been assigned to them, had risen to their feet and were scanning the room for her with desperate eyes.

She waved at them and hurried up to the front of the room, hoping her hair wasn't too wild. She'd just throw her shoulders back, tilt up her chin, and act like she'd meant it all along. It was the only way to go.

Applause swelled as she climbed up onto the stage and joined her team. The master of ceremonies went on with his spiel. "We've just in the past few months had the immense pleasure of learning about the work of Jenna Somers and her amazing team at Arm's Reach.

Now let's watch a video tribute to their passion and dedication that the talented Ava Maddox has prepared for us! Ladies and gentlemen…enjoy!"

The lights went down, the screen lit up and the video began to play.

Twenty-Two

Something was extremely wrong. Drew had been continually texting back to Jenna's frantic message, and she wasn't responding. She wasn't at her place for the dinner either, nor was she at the Arm's Reach table, and now everyone was giving him strange looks, as if they knew something that he didn't.

What the hell? The Wexler Prize was about to be presented, and Jenna was nowhere to be found. Screw this stupid ceremony. He was about to march up on the stage, grab the mic and tell everyone to leave what they were doing and start looking for Jenna when an excited murmur swept over the place.

There. It was her. A flash of light from the brighter corridor outside had spilled into the candlelit ballroom, lighting her up from behind. She'd let her hair down. It was a halo, rimmed with light from the door behind her like a cloud with the sun behind it. She looked wild and gorgeous and sexy. A celestial sky-being. The queen of the night. So damn hot.

Thank God she was okay. Now he could breathe.

She grabbed Vann by the arm, whispered something to him, pressing something into his hand. The murmuring of the crowd got louder.

"…Wexler Prize for Excellence in Biomedical Engineering is awarded to…the Arm's Reach Foundation!"

Drew pushed his way through the ballroom toward her, but Jenna didn't see him. On her trajectory, he wouldn't be able to intercept her before she got up to the dais.

Now she was up on stage with her team. She looked amazing. Her color was high and her eyes sparkled as she scanned the crowd.

The MC carried on with his presentation as Drew forced his way closer to the dais.

"…watch a video tribute to their passion and dedication that the talented Ava Maddox has prepared for us! Ladies and gentlemen…enjoy!"

The lights on the podium dimmed and the screen lit up, but it wasn't the montage of highlights that Ava had compiled from her video series that started to play.

It was a series of photos of him from Arnold Sobel's party. What the *hell*…?

There were gasps all around him. Drew fought the sinking feeling. Cold sweat broke out on his back. He suddenly had the stench of perfume in his nose. The pain of his throbbing head. He looked up at Jenna on the dais.

She wasn't even looking at the photos on the screen behind her. She was looking straight at him. There was no anger or blame or even surprise in her eyes, just a piercing urgency, as if she wanted him to do something, understand something.

He had no idea what, but he was horrified. Whoever was trying to mess with him had chosen the most public moment possible, and was humiliating Jenna in the process. This was her big night to be celebrated for all of her accomplishments, and somehow, Drew had managed to burn it to the ground.

Uncle Malcolm was yelling at him, of course, but Drew couldn't bring himself to listen. He just stared up at the woman he loved, feeling it all slip away.

Uncle Malcolm's words started sinking in. "…turn that thing off, for the love of God! Turn it off!"

"I'm trying to, sir, but I don't know—"

There was a crash, followed by shrieking. Drew looked around. Uncle Malcolm had hurled the laptop down onto the marble tiles. Glass from the screen and letters from the keyboard were scattered all around.

"I've had enough!" his uncle roared. "No more!"

There was another flash of light from the back of the room, and another woman ran into the room, tottering on her high heels. She threw herself at Drew.

"You got me pregnant!" she shrieked.

She was close enough now for him to recognize her. It was the blond woman who had been pictured with him in the tabloid photos, and the ones he'd just seen. The same puffy lips, the same black-rimmed blue eyes, the same streams of mascara running down both her cheeks.

It was the perfume-squirting girl from Arnold Sobel's party.

Pandemonium. Everyone in the room was talking or yelling. Uncle Malcolm could be heard howling above them all. Jenna tried to catch Drew's eye, but now Tina was pounding her fists on Drew's chest. Drew caught her hands and immobilized them, leaning close to speak to her urgently. Whatever he said made her face crumple, and she started to ugly-cry, her mascara cascading down even faster.

"Get out!" Malcolm yelled. "Get this creature out of my sight! And you!" He rounded on Drew, pounding his cane on the floor, his face a dangerously dark red. "You think you can make a fool of me again? I am through with you! You are *done*!"

Drew didn't even respond to his uncle. He just turned his back, looking up at Jenna with a question in his eyes. She could tell that he thought he already knew the answer.

Jenna pulled the mic from the MC'S hand. The man was too startled to yank it back. "It's not his child, Malcolm," Jenna said into the mic. "She was paid to say that."

Malcolm swung around, eyes bulging. "Of course you would cover for him!" he sputtered. "You're in love with him, God help you."

"I have proof." Her voice rang out. "And I want you all to hear it."

Malcolm went still. He slowly turned toward her, his eyes sharpening. The room started quieting down. "What proof are you talking about?" he demanded.

"Vann?" Jenna called out. "Hit it."

There was a buzzy, staticky squeal in the speakers, and the recording began to play. Harold's voice blared out, grinding and nasal.

...we're missing it.

Why do you have to be so mean? Tina's voice, gratingly loud.

The room went silent to listen. The people in that room hung on every word of the bathroom conversation. Tina put her hands on her face, sobbing and shaking her head *no*.

Drew looked up at her, shaking his head. *How?* he mouthed.

Jenna shrugged, which was a very bad idea, considering the precarious state of her décolletage. She grabbed her bodice before it slid down to do a nip slip worthy of a Super Bowl halftime show, and tugged it up, willing it to stay put.

...put your lipstick on! Come on, hurry!"

The click of the bathroom door closing ended the recording. The crowd let out a collective sigh of wonder, and the excited conversation swelled again.

Jenna and Drew couldn't look away from each other. The MC was yelling at her excitedly but Jenna couldn't understand a word the man was saying.

"Harold?" Malcolm roared. "That was Harold on that tape?"

"Yes, it was Harold," Jenna said into the mic. "There he is, slithering away out the southeast door right now! Don't run off, Harold! Some people want a word with you!"

"Stop him!" Malcolm hollered. "That lying bastard has to answer to me!"

Once again, the room erupted into noisy madness. Jenna handed the mic back to the MC. Fortunately, the guy was an old pro, and good at crowd control. He got to work on trying to get the evening somehow back on track, but Jenna couldn't follow his patter. Not with

Drew walking toward the dais, gazing up at her. His whole soul shining out of his eyes.

"…Ms. Somers? Ms. Somers?" The MC again.

"Jenna!" Charles, her team leader, stage-whispered from the back of the dais. "Hey! Jenna, he's calling you! Come and get the prize!"

Somehow, she got herself functioning again. She pasted on a big smile as she went over to receive the prize plaque, and held it up to thunderous applause.

It felt surreal. Far away, like a dream. She made some kind of an acceptance speech. God knows what she said, but the crowd seemed to love it.

So…great. She'd done it. Arm's Reach had the Wexler Prize, in spite of everything. She should feel triumphant, but she couldn't seem to breathe.

In front of the stage, Tina had crumpled to the floor in a dead faint. Pregnancy hormones, guilt, theatrics, who knew. Not Jenna's problem. All she cared about right now was Drew and the dazzled look in his eyes as he gazed up at her.

Afterwards, the rest of the team went back to their table, but she didn't follow. She walked over to the edge of the dais where Drew stood.

He reached up, clasping her waist. She laid both hands on his shoulders as he lifted her and let her slide down his body into a tight, hot embrace. His arms tightened around her, and he put his mouth to her ear.

"That was incredible," he murmured. "Are you okay?"

"Fine," she murmured. "You?"

"Never mind me. I'm so sorry, Jenna. This was your moment to shine. And it got steamrolled."

She shrugged. "I'm fine. I got the prize, right? That's

the important thing. And I kicked Harold's ass, which is very satisfying. So it's all good."

He shook his head, wonderingly. "How in holy hell did you pull that off?"

She wound her arms around him and squeezed. "I got lucky," she said. "Right time, right place."

Drew hugged her back, putting his mouth to her ear. "I want you to know this," he said quietly. "The only reason I was in that bed with those women was because I was drugged. That's not who I am."

She nodded. "Yes," she replied. "I know that."

He let out a sigh of relief. "Thanks," he whispered. "For believing in me."

They just swayed together like a single being, shaking with the intensity of their embrace. Drew looked up. "You know what this means, don't you?"

"It means a whole lot of things," she observed. "Where to even begin?"

"My uncle just fired me," he said. "And I'm fine with that. Finally, things between us are simple, like they should have been from the start. No putting on a show, ever again. I don't need you to save my reputation. I don't want anything except to love you. I don't have anything to offer you but myself."

She pressed her hand to her shaking mouth. "Drew," she whispered.

"Marry me," he said. "For real."

Jenna looked around them, at the crowd of people watching. She laughed out loud.

"You're proposing to me here? In front of everyone?"

Drew's laughter was so happy, she started laughing, too. "Sorry," he said. "I got overexcited and completely forgot they were there. You just have that effect on me."

Jenna wiped her eyes. "I...wow," she whispered.

"Take your time," he said. "As long as you need. I'm not going anywhere, Jenna. I want you to marry me, and I'll spend the rest of my life making damn sure you don't regret it."

"Oh, God, Drew."

Drew glanced around, as if suddenly noticing the ring of people around them, avidly listening. "Maybe some privacy, to talk it over?" he suggested. "We could skip town for a while. I'm a free man now, and your team can cover for you at Arm's Reach for a little while, right? We could blast out of here tonight."

"What?" Uncle Malcolm's voice cut through the murmuring buzz of voices around them. "Who said you were a free man? Who said you could blast out of town?"

"You just banished me, Uncle," Drew pointed out. "I think that means I can go."

"Oh, don't be childish," Malcolm said gruffly. "I wasn't myself. You're not going anywhere. You're my CEO!"

"Actually, you weren't invited into this conversation at all," Drew told him.

Ava stepped forward. She blew Jenna a kiss, her eyes shining, and then murmured into her uncle's ear in low, soothing tones, leading him firmly away.

Drew turned back to her, and when their eyes met, that magical bubble reformed around them. They were surrounded by people, but they might as well have been alone.

Drew rested his forehead against hers. "Now, from the top," he said. "Shall we go find someplace private so I can try this whole marriage proposal thing again?"

Jenna laughed through her tears. "How about if I just save us some time and say hell yes right now, so we can skip ahead to the good part?"

His reply was a kiss of such molten intensity, neither of them even heard the appreciative roar of applause that shook the room. It could have been miles away.

All that mattered was the two of them together. The road ahead, to parts unknown.

And the love, lighting their way.

* * * * *

Don't miss the next
Men of Maddox Hill novel
Corner Office Secrets
by New York Times *bestselling author*
Shannon McKenna
Available June 2021
From Harlequin Desire.

COMING NEXT MONTH FROM

DESIRE

Available April 13, 2021

#2797 THE MARRIAGE HE DEMANDS
Westmoreland Legacy: The Outlaws by Brenda Jackson
Wealthy Alaskan Cash Outlaw has inherited a ranch and needs land owned by beautiful, determined Brianna Banks. She'll sign it over with one condition: Cash fathering the child she desperately wants. But he won't be an absentee father and makes his own demand...

#2798 BLUE COLLAR BILLIONAIRE
Texas Cattleman's Club: Heir Apparent • by Karen Booth
After heartbreak, socialite Lexi Alderidge must focus on her career, not another relationship. But she makes an exception for the rugged worker at her family's construction site, Jack Bowden. Sparks fly, but is he the man she's assumed he is?

#2799 CONSEQUENCES OF PASSION
Locketts of Tuxedo Park • by Yahrah St. John
Heir to a football dynasty, playboy Roman Lockett is used to getting what he wants, but one passionate night with Shantel Wilson changes everything. Overwhelmed by his feelings, he tries to forget her—until he learns she's pregnant. Now he vows to claim his child...

#2800 TWIN GAMES IN MUSIC CITY
Dynasties: Beaumont Bay • by Jules Bennett
When music producer Will Sutherland signs country's biggest star, Hannah Banks, their mutual attraction is way too hot...so she switches with her twin to avoid him. But Will isn't one to play games—or let a scheming business rival ruin everything...

#2801 SIX NIGHTS OF SEDUCTION
by Maureen Child
CEO Noah Graystone cares about business and nothing else. Tired of being taken for granted, assistant Tessa Parker puts in her notice—but not before one last business trip with no-strings seduction on the schedule. Can their six hot nights turn into forever?

#2802 SO RIGHT...WITH MR. WRONG
The Serenghetti Brothers • by Anna DePalo
Independent fashion designer Mia Serenghetti needs the help of Damian Musil—son of the family that has been feuding with hers for years. But when one hot kiss leads to a passion neither expected, what will become of these star-crossed lovers?

YOU CAN FIND MORE INFORMATION ON UPCOMING HARLEQUIN TITLES, FREE EXCERPTS AND MORE AT HARLEQUIN.COM.

HDCNM0321

"Are you really going to sell the Blazing Frontier without
even taking the time to look at it? It's a beautiful place."

"I'm sure it is, but I have no need of a ranch, dude or
otherwise."

"I think you're making a mistake, Cash."

Cash lifted a brow. Normally, he didn't care what any
person, man or woman, thought about any decision he made,
but for some reason what she thought mattered.

It shouldn't.

What he should do was thank her for joining him for
lunch, and tell her not to walk back to Cavanaugh's office
with him, although he knew both their cars were parked there.
In other words, he should put as much distance between them
as possible.

I can't.

Maybe it was the way her luscious mouth tightened when
she was not happy about something. He'd picked up on it
twice now. Lord help him but he didn't want to see it a third
time. He'd rather see her smile, lick an ice cream cone or...
lick him.

HDEXP0321

He quickly forced the last image from his mind, but not before a hum of lust shot through his veins. There had to be a reason he was so attracted to her. Maybe he could blame it on the Biggins deal Garth had closed just months before he'd gotten engaged to Regan. That had taken working endless days and nights, and for the past year Cash's social life had been practically nonexistent.

On the other hand, even without the Biggins deal as an excuse, there was strong sexual chemistry radiating between them. He felt it but honestly wasn't sure that even at twenty-seven she recognized it for what it was.

That was intriguing, to the point that he was tempted to hang around Black Crow another day. Besides, he was a businessman, and no businessman would sell or buy anything without checking it out first. He was letting his personal emotions around Ellen cloud what was usually a very sound business mind.

"You are right, Brianna. I would be making a mistake if I didn't at least see the ranch before selling it. Is now a good time?"

The huge smile that spread across her face was priceless… and mesmerizing. When was the last time a woman, any woman, had this kind of effect on him? When he felt spellbound? He concluded that never had a woman captivated him like Brianna Banks was doing.

Don't miss what happens next in
The Marriage He Demands
by Brenda Jackson, the next book in her
Westmoreland Legacy: The Outlaws series!

Available April 2021 wherever
Harlequin Desire books and ebooks are sold.

Harlequin.com

Don't miss the next book in the sexy and irresistible Jackson Falls series by

SYNITHIA WILLIAMS

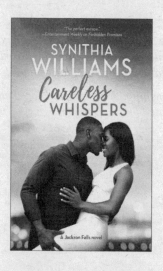

"Williams (*His Pick for Passion*) makes waves with this exceptional tale of forbidden love."
—*Publishers Weekly*, starred review, on *Forbidden Promises*

Order your copy today!

PHSWBPA0321

SPECIAL EXCERPT FROM

HQN

Return to Jackson Falls for the next sexy and irresistible book in Synithia Williams's reader-favorite series featuring the Robidoux family!

When everything is working to keep them apart, can these two former enemies learn to trust one another for a chance at forever?

Read on for a sneak peek at
Careless Whispers

She turned to face him, her heart pounding again and a dozen warning bells going off in her head. She should shut down the flirting, but the look in Alex's eyes said he was willing to go with her down this path. "I've got some experience with wanting the wrong man."

"But that's all in your past now." He took a half step closer.

She shook her head. She'd never been good at not going for what she wanted. Her ego needed stroking, and Alex with his quiet understanding and empathy had shown her more care than anyone had in a long time. She'd be smarter this time. This was just to quell her curiosity. People said there was a thin line between love and hate. Maybe all their bickering had just been leading to this.

"Not quite," she said, choosing her next words carefully. She pretended to check the list in her box. "I find myself thinking about someone who I once despised. I miss clashing with him daily. I enjoy the verbal sparring. Not to mention he recently wrapped his arms around me, and for some reason I can't get that out of my head." She glanced at him. "He's stronger than I imagined. His embrace comforting in a way I didn't realize I'd like. It makes me want more even though I know I shouldn't."

Alex stilled next to her. "What are you going to do about this ill-advised craving?"

"It kind of depends on him," she said. "I think he's interested, but I can't be sure. And you know I can never offer myself to a man who didn't want me." She said the last part with a slight shrug. Though her heart imitated a hummingbird flitting against her ribs, and a mixture of excitement and adrenaline flowed with each beat.

Alex slid closer, closing the distance between them and filling her senses with him. He pulled the paper out of her hands. "What if he wants you, too?"

His deep voice slid over her like warm satin. She faced him and met his dark eyes. "Then I'm in trouble, because I'm no good at saying no to the things I want but shouldn't have."

Don't miss what happens next in...
Careless Whispers *by Synithia Williams.*

Available March 2021 wherever
HQN books and ebooks are sold.

HQNBooks.com